WHEN YOU HAD POWER

NOTHING IS PROMISED 1

SUSAN KAYE QUINN

www.SusanKayeQuinn.com

Cover by BZN Studios

ISBN: 9798567127919

———————

For better, for worse. In sickness and in health.

It's a legal vow of care for families in 2050, a world beset by
waves of climate-driven plagues.

Power engineer Lucía Ramirez long ago lost her family to one—
she'd give anything to take that vow. The Power Islands give
humanity a fighting chance, but tending kelp farms and solar lilies
is a lonely job. The housing AI found her a family match, saying
she should fit right in with the Senegalese retraining expert who's
a force of nature, the ex-Pandemic Corps cook with his own cozy
channel, and even the writer who insists everything is stories, all
the way down. This family of literal and metaphorical refugees
could be the shelter she's seeking from her own personal storm.

She *needs* this one to work.

Then an unscheduled power outage and a missing turtle-bot

crack open a mystery. Something isn't right on Power Island One, but every step she takes to solve it, someone else gets there first— and they're determined to make her unsee what she's seen. Lucía is an engineer, not a detective, but fixing this problem might cost her the one thing she truly needs: *a home.*

When You Had Power is the first of four tightly-connected novels in a new hopepunk series. It's about our future, how society will shift and flex like a solar lily in the storms of our own making, and how breaks in the social fabric have to be expected, tended to, and healed. Because we're in this together, now more than ever before.

ONE

A STEAMING PLUME OF ANTI-VIRAL SPRAY doused her.

Lucía held her breath until the gas settled on the concrete step below her boots. The biohaz goggles were definitely the right call. Nothing like blasting off any freeloading virus before saying hello. She hitched her backpack and smiled for the camera, wherever it was. The cottage-sized house was like a fairy tale—a literal white-picket-fence, beautiful bay windows (blinds closed; sorry, no sneak previews), and a tiny garden with responsibly-California-native wildflowers and an inviting wooden bench.

Two ceramic frogs were making out on the seat.

Then there was the half-inch-thick acrylic shield

sealing off the porch. Probably could survive a sarin gas attack if their Huntington Beach homeowner's association went Mad Max over the frogs. She focused on the house number and tapped the display hovering in the air just past her goggles. Her chip brought up the overlay. *The Strong Family.* Yup, this was the right place.

"Hello, Lucía Ramirez. Do I have your name right?" The household bot spoke from a hidden speaker, basically asking for a voice print. No sign of the family inside, but the bot's non-gendered face appeared on the shield, patiently awaiting her answer.

Lucía carefully lifted the goggles from her eyes and perched them on her forehead, in case the bot wanted a facial scan as well. She took care not to lick her lips or rub the itch on her nose. She had no problem with the borderline-non-consensual anti-viral dosing—she was determined to make this whole thing go smoothly—but practically speaking, that shit hurt if it got on your mucous membranes.

"Yes, I'm Lucía Ramirez." She annunciated clearly, maintaining the pretense she was having a conversation not passing a security check. This was part of the interview, to be sure. And if you couldn't even be polite to a house bot... The Southern California Housing Authority's AI gave this family match a 95% rating, which was crazy high. Lucía had filled out the application. She'd received an invite. But this was the final step. The literal crossing over the threshold. You weren't in until you were in. And even then, it would be probationary for weeks, months, or even years. No commitment, no legal papers until everyone was on board. Which only made sense. Anyone could tell a good story with their public-facing data, and her application was as genuine as recorded media allowed, but reality lay in true face-to-face interactions. That's when you discovered if the AI had found a real match. Or if you brushed your teeth too loudly and had to be kicked out. "If this is a bad time, I can come back later." She tried not to sound desperate. Because she wasn't, not strictly. She could always find a place to stay. She just didn't have a *home*.

"Oh, no, honey, you're right on time." A roundish human face, light brown skin with deep brown eyes, had taken the bot's place. He smiled wide, and it seemed warm, as much as you could tell on the flatness of the house shield.

"*What*—she needs to show her—" A second man

shooed the first off-screen then scowled at her. He was leaner, his expression cooler. "We need to see your passport first. Sorry."

"No, it's fine." She hustled to pull the thin paper booklet out of her backpack pocket. The front page had all the latest vaccine stamps. She pressed it against the transparent shield, lining it up with the front door, uncertain exactly where the camera lay.

"Scan document," the man instructed the bot. Lucía held extra still for the split second of scan. The man was pale-skinned, mid-thirties. He had to be Jex, one half of the core couple of the family. She'd read their profiles, of course, when she applied—Jex and Wicket Strong—two of the six people in the cottage. Seven, if Lucía was adopted in. The rest were peripherals like her, their profiles not accessible, at least not with a locator, for safety. The Strongs were the gatekeepers, deciding who would be let in.

Who fit in. They were the human fit-check.

The Housing Authority's AI was like a digital oracle—no one understood how it pattern-matched all that data and popped out a match, but everyone used the predictions anyway. Except that humans, while absurdly predictable on average, were impossible to model individually. And they weren't stable systems. A family match was more like a weather prediction. Probably sunny... but still a 10% chance of thunderstorms. Because even when you didn't annoy the crap out of each other, even when you thought you were accepted into a family, when an unstable low-pressure front came through, things didn't always work out as planned.

Which was why she was here.

"Got my latest shots just a couple days ago," she offered. She'd already given them access to all her public-facing med records. Jex was obviously scouring the scan, probably checking it against the digital copy. "Rota-49," she added. That was the big outbreak last year, but the vaccine had just become available. It was only June, but 2050 had already been a banner year for ancient viruses and bacteria. They rose in unending waves from what used to be the permafrost, like old gods summoned to punish humans for their poor choices and petroleum usage. Humanity had made strides in the climate crisis, but not enough. Fires kept burning, arable land was still shrinking, and the sea continued to rage, warming-driven storms pounding the land and reclaiming sections of it every year. Which meant refugees—animal and human—constantly encroaching on each other's domains, creating the perfect breeding ground for every imaginable crossover virus. And nature was very imaginative. It was a constant race between each new pandemic sweeping the globe and the World Science Organization's vaccine trials to defeat it. "Oh, and the new pox shot," she tagged on while Jex kept scrutinizing her passport. He may have heard of it. The WSO's alert system had just identified a 10,000-year-old smallpox variant in Canada.

The afternoon sun was drying the layer of antiviral mist on her skin, which made that itch on her nose impossible to ignore. She took a quick swipe at it with her glove.

Wicket's face squished back onto the screen. "Oh! Do they have that vaccine out already?"

"Just released." Lucía smiled. She had early access, on account of her work. "Probably Phase 5, essential workers only. But it's an orthopoxvirus—I guess close enough to standard smallpox that they could rapid-release. I got the shot coming back to the mainland." It was actually a Phase 4 clinical trial, not yet approved for the public, but she didn't want to add that to the mix. Her mother always said if you were healthy, be first in line—but you never knew how people would react to that sort of thing.

"See?" Wicket tapped Jex's shoulder in a triumphant way. "I told you. Power engineer. They're the best."

Jex narrowed his eyes. Wicket whisked off-screen, but Lucía heard his "Let her in!" loud and clear.

She suppressed her smile but tucked her passport away.

Jex's scowl doubled down. "We've got a strict schedule of chore rotation. I hope you don't mind cleaning bathrooms."

"Of course. I'll only be here two weeks at a time, then four weeks working on the Island. But I'm happy to do extra when I'm, uh, at the cottage." She didn't want to say *home*—not when they hadn't even let her on the porch.

"Rotations on cooking, too." He pursed his lips.

"I grew up in a big family, back in Puerto Rico. Everyone cooked."

He nodded. It looked approving. "And no anti-chippers. Not even as guests."

"Understood." She had an implanted interface just below her temple for accessing the net, like most people—she wasn't one of the fanatics who thought strapping the chip *outside* their head made some kind of mystical difference. Her chip had the stan-

7

dard sensory integration plus a few enhancements and a waterproof base station in her pack, but that was a little... *extra*. Not something you bragged about.

Jex squinted, leaned closer to the screen, and dropped his voice. "Dodgers or Angels?"

"Is that... sports?" She didn't follow sports. Any of them. *Shit.*

He waved that off. "Never mind."

Her heart lurched, but then she realized he meant *never mind the question* not *get off my porch*.

Jex sighed and studied her for a moment. "Look. We're happy here, all right? We don't need to fill this slot. Things are good. So, if you've got some trouble I need to know about, well, I need to know about it."

A loosening through Lucía's hunched-up shoulders made them drop. This was it. He knew she'd transferred from her assignment up north—from Oregon's Power Island 43 down to the historic Power Island One, just off the Southern California coast. It was on her application, an entirely reasonable excuse to be seeking a new family. She thought she might at least make it inside before having to spill the real reason. Or part of it, anyway.

She could lie. But she couldn't live that way, not and hope to find a real home again.

"I had some troubles at work."

It wasn't a pretty story. Especially given power engineers still carried that "hero" label. The world was desperate to reduce the warming of the planet— the cost in lives grew every year—and humanity's true lifeblood was electricity. The Power Islands were *net negative*—they supplied green energy to power most of the county, and they were CO_2 sinks as well. No one wanted to know some of those engineering heroes had a dark side.

"What kind of troubles?" The edge to Jex's voice said he'd seen *real* problems. The kind he had no intention of letting in his home.

She had no idea where this would fall on his spectrum of bad news. "One of my co-workers was stalking me."

Jex's expression opened up, and he was clearly all-ears for more.

Lucía shifted, the peeling anti-viral film just adding to the discomfort. "Four weeks on the Island is a lot of time. He got the wrong idea about things." *Ugh.* It sounded like she was defending him. "The thing is, I wasn't the first."

Jex's disgust wasn't aimed at her. "They never do it just once, do they?"

The knot in her stomach loosened. "No. But my

co-workers didn't believe me. Or my boss. I had to gather evidence, basically stalking my stalker. It was a mess until I finally went to the regional director."

"And they made *you* leave?" Jex's ire zoomed up. It warmed her face. She hadn't had anyone defend her, even in the abstract, not since she moved to the mainland for school.

"No, no, I..." This was where it got awkward. She was still standing on the step, spilling all this, which somehow made it worse. "He was transferred out. To an arctic station, I believe. Somewhere he couldn't prey on anyone else. Plus, he got mandated remote therapy."

"*That's* what I'm talking about!" Jex jabbed a righteous finger at her on the display.

She laughed a little then cleared her throat. "But the other power engineers, they all rallied around him. Even the designer—our boss," she clarified. "I requested the transfer. I just couldn't be in a place where people didn't have my back." Which was the truth, but only half of it. The rest was just too... she'd have to ease into sharing that part. After she got past the front door.

"Well, of course not!" Jex's indignation fizzled as he seemed to realize she was still standing on the step. "Well, what are you doing out there? Come on in."

The acrylic shield zipped to the side, granting her access to the porch. The relief gushed through her so hard, she stumbled the three steps to the door. It was open before she got there. Jex stepped aside as she crossed the threshold. He towered over her with a slim yet muscular build. His sternness had softened enough to make him not too intimidating. His short sleeve t-shirt revealed a military-style tattoo. She only got a glimpse, but the caduceus was clear—the twined snakes of the Pandemic Corps. So, he'd served.

Lucía met his steady gaze. That wasn't on his profile.

"Finally!" Wicket scurried into the entranceway from a side room filled with chairs and a couch. He was more round in body and face than Jex, with black stud earrings in both ears that resembled tiny circuit boards. "What took you so long?"

Lucía wasn't sure who he was chastising, but Jex seemed to know. "I had questions."

"You always have questions." Wicket pressed his hands together and made a short bow. "Welcome to our home, Ms. Ramirez."

She grinned and namasted back. "It's nice to make it past the porch."

Wicket scowled. "Did you tell her about cozy time?" he demanded of Jex.

"If I had a minute—"

Wicket *hrumpfed*, and that's when it hit her—they were like Benita and Luis, her tía and tío, harassing one another so hard, you could miss that they'd be lost without each other. Lucía worked back a surge of hope. It was way too early to be thinking of them like her Puerto Rican familia. She was barely in the door.

Wicket waved her toward the stairs. "No more questions. Girl needs a shower—those anti-virals are hell on hair, and yours is too gorgeous to let anything happen. You need to clean up before cozy time. Come on." He guided her while carefully avoiding any touch. Which she expected. They'd be sharing air in the small cottage, that couldn't be helped, but crossing that next barrier would take some time. And she was due to start at Power Island One on Monday, which left only a day and a half to get acquainted.

"Cozy time?" she asked Wicket as he led the way up the stairs. Jex had shaken his head and drifted toward the adjacent dining room—the one hidden behind the bay windows—and a kitchen that peeked from around the corner.

"It's *sacred,* so you have to show up," Wicket was saying. "Jex didn't tell you?"

She shook her head. The stairs creaked. The yellow of the walls warmed with the sun, which leaked from a small window at the end of the hall. Bedrooms lined it, two on a side, with control pads on the wall.

Wicket focused on one, tapped the air above the keypad, then explained, "You've got access now. Just program your own key."

She did so, quickly, using the air-touch interface as well. No need to show off her CBT—control-by-thought—upgrade. Her new access code would store automatically in her key manager. She tested it, and the door clicked unlocked.

Wicket bustled through, and Lucía hovered at the threshold—it was even more storybook on the inside. Sunny yellow walls and shiny hardwood floors. Pristine, fluffy-white bedspread heaped with extra pillows and blankets. Gauzy linen drapes softly billowing in front of white paned windows. Far warmer and more inviting than her room in Oregon. Her work pants, boots, and bedraggled backpack felt like they sullied it, muddy footprints tracked into a palace.

She actually glanced at the floor to check, then quickly stepped into the room.

Wicket was pulling towels out of the closet and setting them on the bed.

She packed light—the Island provided most of what she needed, and she shipped her tools directly there. Her backpack was her life. Scuffed old-tech nylon, four strap repairs in 17 years, housing three outfits, a toothbrush, her mama's hairbrush, and a tiny octopus named Ollie, which was made of black satin and slithered in your hand. He was buckled in one of the pockets for safety. She set her backpack carefully on the floor next to the bed, trying not to touch anything with it, and debated rapidly whether she should take off her shoes. Wicket had bare feet and comfortable clothes, but he *lived* here.

Maybe she did too. For a while, at least.

She kept her shoes on.

Next to the bed, on a spindly wooden table, sat a delicate white teacup, still steaming, and an empanadilla that had to be fresh by the mouth-watering look of the fried crust and the savory smell.

"Did you..." She worked to get the right tone. Amazed? Grateful? A flood of feelings suffused her.

"Did you make this just for me?" It sounded small, but she couldn't help it.

"*Me?* Oh, heck no!" Wicket waved that off as he scurried to adjust the windows, cutting down on the breeze. "Anything *cozy* is Jex. He has a channel, you know. *The Easy Pleaser.* Over a million watchers now. He's got a real gift for it. I just code AI for the corporate overlords and try not to burn the pancakes."

Lucía's grin was slow in coming, but she felt it through her whole body.

Wicket turned down the covers of the bed and fluffed the pillows in an awkward way, like he wasn't sure what he was doing. "Bathroom's down the hall," he said, giving up on that. "Afraid you have to share with everyone on the floor, but there's a schedule for that." He swiped the air quickly, and a message popped up on her display with an invite. *A shower calendar.* She could work with that. "If there's anything you need, just message me." He was already at the door. "Cozy time is just after sunset, or whenever Amaal is done with prayers." He waved the air again, brushing that away. "You'll meet her and everyone then. Settle in!"

And he was gone.

She let her gaze soak in the room one more time

then wandered over to the window. The ocean breeze carried even though they were a mile from the coast. The city haze had been swept away, leaving the sky clean and blue. She closed her eyes briefly, breathing it in. Flashes of memory lit up her mind. Her childhood bedroom window where the ocean breeze was always knocking. The sun's warmth on her face when she opened it to a brand-new day. Even the background smell of the empanadilla spiced her memories of home.

She opened her eyes to the normal glint of the city. It wasn't her childhood Island home, but it was dangerously close. That surged up too much hope— the fragile kind that could easily shatter. And she'd taken a lot of hits lately.

She pulled in another lungful of salty air, then turned from the window and swiped through to sign up for a shower slot. Unpacking took two minutes, including peeling off her gloves and stowing her biohaz goggles, but before she could gather her things to wash up, a message came through, hovering in her peripheral vision, demanding attention. She gave in and flicked it open.

It was from Tito, her cousin. *Are you settled with the new familia?*

She summoned a virtual keyboard and typed back. *Yes. And they made empanadillas.*

¡Wepa! Wait, is this some trick? Maybe they are a front for some LA gang that's luring in pretty Boricua girls with delicious treats.

Definitely. Probably have to kill someone after cozy time. She repacked her backpack with shower things.

What is that? A code word? What are these Californians getting you into?

She grabbed the empanadilla and blinked a picture, sending it off to Tito. Then she took a bite—it tasted even better than it looked.

Tito's response flashed back. *Whoa. That is one beautiful empanadilla.*

I will gladly kill for food this good. She took another bite, too soon, greedy for it in a way that felt risky. She needed to rein all this back in. *See? They're good people. Have to go, Tito. Don't come rescue me.*

You need to come rescue me! Abuela is making a million pasteles tonight, and you know she won't let us rest until they're done. I will probably die tonight. Light a candle for me. But then his message faded. In Puerto Rico, it seemed like every family was *big*. And *loud*. Tías, tíos, primos—she had been adopted into so many familias, it seemed like she was related to everyone left in the state. And there was always someone checking up on her. She had to fight to keep them out of her business. It was bustling and loving and wonderful.

And she left it all behind to chase after a dream.

Just like her parents, she'd come to the mainland for school. They'd met at Stanford, but that was back before the Power Engineering Institute became the premier place for engineers to receive their training. So Lucía applied to the one in LA. Being legacy of Energy Island engineers helped her get in. Her parents had married after graduation and had started their family right away. That was the first hit—for her, dating at the Institute was a few frantic affairs, but nothing solid. Nothing to build a family on. Her parents had moved to Power Island One when she was three, and her first memories were there. Those days were as bright and gauzy as the yellow linen drapes billowing gently in her room. But when she graduated and went to Oregon, the second hit came —none of it was the same. Maybe the Islands were never that way in reality. She couldn't honestly be sure. Maybe her memories were a story she told herself after the plague took them, her parents first, and then her brothers. That ancient virus made the world truly desperate—and the waves kept coming after that. Her family had been wiped away in a blink, like so many others. Her familia in Puerto Rico cared for her, but those memories of her parents and brothers, her first family, were her bedrock. They were the cliff she stood on, holding out against the rising sea, stronger than all of nature's fury... only it turned out the bluff was made of sandstone, appearing solid but slowly eroding with each crashing wave, threatening to slip into the sea. Reality was pandemics and creepy co-workers and long, lonely shifts... and a mainland home that had been no such thing in the end.

She was here, at Jex and Wicket's, *trying again,* because she still clung to the dream.

Was that foolish... or the only thing that mattered?

She eased off her boots, sat on the edge of the bed, and finished the empanadilla while nursing the tea. By the time it was gone, the fatigue of just getting into the house, the pull of the plush pillows and cool sheets was more than she could resist. Shower could wait. Besides, a nap would power her up again for "cozy time," whatever that might be. This could be a home, a real one if she could hold onto it. She simply had to not mess it up. And hope that the fairy tale wasn't too good to be true. She bumped her shower out a couple hours then drifted off, thinking how she didn't have much time to earn her place on this tiny island of softness. *Just a day...*

Out of a dead sleep, an alert roused her, beeping in her ear and saying she was late for cozy time. The street lights had come on, coloring the room orange. She'd missed the shower slot altogether. She asked the lights to turn on, then scrambled to get her stuff, nearly slipping in her stocking feet as she hustled out into the hall. The tiny bathroom was empty, so she twisted her hair up into a knot and jumped in the shower. The controls were manual, and it took her a minute to figure them out. The residual anti-viral washed off her skin easily. She decided to wash her hair, just in case Wicket might notice. The lights flickered, just once, which made her freeze mid-rinse. Outages were tightly scheduled. Had she slept through an alert? Maybe the flicker was just water in her eyes. But if Jex and Wicket had a bad breaker, she might have a chance to be useful right away. She was a power engineer, not an electrician, but she could be handy around the house. Prove her worth.

She finished washing her hair and then rinsed off. Just as she reached for a towel—

The lights went out.

The bathroom was utter blackness.

What the hell? She definitely hadn't missed the ten-minute alert that always preceded an outage. People had to have time—to make sure their backups were functioning, especially for critical med equipment and emergency bot services, even just to finish recharging your chip before a surge came through. There had to be something wrong with the breaker—

A terrified wail pierced the dark.

TWO

Lucía quickly dried off then searched for her clothes in the dark.

The wail went on and on, but it was broken by gasps for air, and by the time she was dressed, she recognized it as a baby's cry. She felt her way out of the bathroom and down the hall—her base station, with its built-in light, was in her room, next to the empty teacup. She inched her way through the blackness, fingertips grazing the wall to keep grounded—even the streetlights must be out, or they'd have lit up her room. Which raised the hairs on her arms. *What the hell was happening?* She gingerly felt along the nightstand but still managed to knock the teacup over before she found her base station.

The baby's cry paused just long enough to hear the smash of china against the hardwood floor.

"Shit." She found the base station and clicked on the light, only then remembering she could have remote-accessed it through her chip. But when she tried to bring up a connection, she was offline. The base station was working, which meant... she killed the light and peered out the window. Everything was dark as far as she could see. Were the gateways down too? Online access was as fundamental a utility as power—every gateway should automatically switch to backup power before a scheduled outage. In the rare event backups failed on one, there were a dozen more gateways within range. *How could everything be down?*

Footsteps in the hall hurried toward her room, a light bouncing ahead of them.

Jex appeared in her doorway. "You okay?" he demanded, his base station beam blinding her then dropping to the broken teacup at her feet.

"I'm so sorry." Lucía crouched to pick it up, but it was shattered. The three main pieces were surrounded by a debris field of tiny slivers. "It was an accident. I'll replace it, I promise!" She had to raise her voice to be heard over the crying baby. She gathered the large pieces in her hand, but the shards were impossible. She tried anyway.

"That's all it was?" Jex's hand on her elbow tugged her to standing. She obliged, awkwardly cradling the pieces and her base station, heart pounding. His light blinded her again as he scanned her. "I thought maybe you'd fallen."

"I'm fine."

"What?" He couldn't hear her over the baby.

"I'm fine!" she shouted just as the crying stopped. Her voice echoed, and she cringed, but Jex didn't seem fazed.

A light outside her window went on, but it wasn't a street lamp—a second-floor window in one of the tidy cottages shone light on the street.

"What's happening?" It didn't make any sense—the whole area should have power.

"I thought maybe *you* would know."

She whipped her gaze back to him, but he was serious. Her heart shrank. She was a power engineer. Of course, she should know what was happening.

"That," he waved at the lit-up cottage, "is the Hampton's solar backup coming on. Amaal should be hooking ours up any moment."

She frowned. "Aren't your backups automatic?"

Every building had a mandated solar battery backup system that would kick on during the scheduled outages. Sometimes they failed, so it was always good to check before the outage started—hence the alerts.

Windows lit up in two more houses across the street.

"Let's get back downstairs." Jex tipped his head and waved his base light, beckoning her out of the room. Lucía set the broken cup pieces on the bedside table, stuffed her base station in her pocket, and followed. Jex explained further as they shuffled down the hall to the top of the steps. "Lately, we've had to disconnect the backups. When the power goes out, there's no alert. Nothing. Just flickers and a sudden surge. I've got two blown battery packs to prove it. But these outages are something crazy—they drain down everything. Like they're sucking the power right out. If you have backups connected to the grid, it'll empty those in a flash, and you'll have nothing left. So, we keep them disconnected."

"That's... really strange." It was crazy talk. Absolute conspiracy-theory trash, but she didn't want to say that.

"Like I was saying." Jex held up his light so it illuminated the stairs.

Her mind raced as they carefully made their way down. It *was* true that the grid tapped customer backups when more power was needed to match the load, but that wasn't commonly known. And if that had happened here, it would have been spread out so only a trickle would have been pulled from each building.... definitely not draining a whole neighborhood of batteries at once. But *something* weird was going on. Power was critical. Outages were scheduled. Universal backups existed precisely so this wouldn't happen.

They'd reached the entranceway and crossed to the living room, which had two figures, their lights casting a dance of shadows on the walls. Wicket waved away Jex's light and shushed them, silently, one figure to his lips, while he held a baby. She was no good with baby ages, having not spent much time around them, but the source of the unholy wailing was now a little angel with tear-streaked soft-brown cheeks.

A young woman hovered nearby, probably the mother. She had the same soft-brown skin, like a lot of light-skinned Latinas in LA with some long-ago Mexican ancestor. The baby's dark-haired head was solidly slumped on Wicket's shoulder. If he weren't wearing the same black wedding band as Jex, she would have thought maybe Wicket was the father—both in appearance and the sure rhythm he had with the baby, rocking her with his whole body, moving side-to-side. A surrogate, maybe? Not that it was any of Lucía's business, but she *was* curious. If nothing else, just to understand how everybody fit.

"You always have the touch," the mother said. "I can take her upstairs."

"You hold the light," Wicket said, gesturing with his chin as he eased into rocking toward the stairs.

The woman gave Lucía an apologetic smile then led the way.

Jex waited until they were halfway up the stairs. "That's Maria and her baby, Eva," he said in a hushed tone. "Not the way I'd hoped you'd meet. How are you with babies?"

"I was kind of always the baby myself." That got a pinched response. "But I'm happy to help out," she quickly added.

He nodded approval.

That was part of the deal in joining a family—you contributed some of your income, but more importantly, you took care of each other. Not just chores, but everything. *In sickness and in health.* Which mattered a lot when you never knew which plague would roll through next. Everyone had access to the med centers and treatments, but *care* was a lot more than that. And babies were a *lot* of care.

Back in Puerto Rico, she really was the baby. *Still.* Birth rates were dramatically down everywhere, especially in places in the thick of the climate-crisis—islands like Puerto Rico and hot zone spots around the planet's middle were shrinking in population. Children had become increasingly rare. The planet still had plenty of humans, although fewer every year. She often felt like she was the end of an era, her birth twenty-five years ago marking the beginning of the end of worries about runaway over-population. It couldn't be that strange for someone not to have baby care experience—it would definitely be new for her.

A flurry of alerts flashed up on her display.

Jex had to have received them too. "Good, the gateway backups are online."

Lucía flicked away the alerts, one after another. They were all internal systems checks, the type her chip ran after losing connection, which was rare. None of the alerts said anything about the power outage. More houses outside were getting power back, but still no street lamps.

Suddenly, the living room lit up. Lucía squinted against the glare, then startled when she noticed another person in the room. In the front corner, near the windows to the porch, a white guy, mid-twenties, was perched on an upholstered chair. His legs were folded on the seat, hands on his knees, not making a sound—his ears were blocked with mute plugs, and his eyes were covered with light-blocking goggles. *Ultra Black.* She'd seen them before. A standard chip fed overlays to your optic nerve—to go virtual, you needed to block out reality, and the goggles and plugs got you there. With CBT and a few upgrades, you could go full immersion. She couldn't tell what mode this guy was in, but he was as still as the dead.

"That's Joe," Jex explained, clicking off his base station light. "He's probably running offline, just on his base. Says he doesn't like to be connected when he's playing. Power's too unreliable." He gave her a sideways look that felt like a demand for explanation.

Only Lucía had none to give.

Before she was forced to confess that, a striking Black woman strode through a door at the end of the room. Lucía glimpsed the kitchen just beyond as the door swung shut.

"I don't know how much we have!" The woman threw her hands up in the air as if Lucía and Jex had just interrogated her. She was dressed in a vibrant orange-and-gold suit with an elaborate headwrap that swirled and tied up her hair.

Jex frowned. "The battery should be fully charged."

The woman gestured to him with one hand. "Yes, it *should*. And yet the indicator is at half, maybe two-thirds capacity." Her accent was strong —*cap-a-sah-TEE* was precisely enunciated with the emphasis at the end.

"Maybe I could take a look?" Lucía offered.

"Ah, could you? How wonderful." A wide smile blossomed on her face. "And you are the new one! Wicket told me you'd come today. Welcome." She spread her arms wide and gathered up Lucía in a hug. She was so startled, she kind of froze. It was short, and before she could react, the woman had pulled back and pressed her hands together, bowing for a more normal greeting.

Lucía hastened to return it.

"This is Amaal Sayed," Jex said, although he was stiff about it. "I'm sure I can take a look at the battery, Amaal. We don't have to bother our guest about it."

Guest. That stung. Like she was still out on the porch in Jex's mind.

"Of course, you're right." But Amaal didn't seem

too convinced. "We shouldn't make her work right away." Her smile was still abundantly warm.

"Amaal is from Senegal—"

"He means I am a *refugee*. Go ahead and say it, Jex!"

"I didn't think—"

"Ach!" She dismissed him with a wave and leaned a bit toward Lucía. "He is a little timid for a man who runs an entire household."

"*Timid?*" Jex's affront was almost comical.

Amaal's pitying look made it worse. "Oh, come now. Admit it. You are *soft-hearted*. You think with kindness. It is a good thing. You know what I mean!" Then she waved the air as if that brushed it all away. Jex looked like she'd just broadcast his half-naked baby pictures, bragged about how adorable he was to the world, and now he was paralyzed by the horror. And too stunned to object.

Lucía kept her lips buttoned.

"I have been here five years now," Amaal breezed on as if Jex weren't dying right next to her. "In Senegal, I was a teacher, but my town dried up. Then I got a ticket in the refugee raffle, so it was then or never. I came straight to LA, and Jex and Wicket brought me in, their first family member! They helped me get my feet under me."

"So, what do you do now?" Lucía tried to float the conversation while Jex was still recovering from the devastation.

"I am a retraining expert," Amaal said with a slight bow as if introducing herself as the Queen of Senegal. "The climate crisis keeps me very much in demand. And then there is the displacement from automation. But all the AI in the world cannot do what the lowliest refugee can, no matter what trials the world may have held for them."

"What's that?" Lucía asked. She was already on board, and she didn't even know the answer.

"Use the brain God gave you!" Amaal spoke with her hands, arms, and elbows. Fingers splayed for emphasis. "Explore! Create! Have courage! You have to try. Don't give up. You need to dig down and find the part that *cares*. Being able to care is deeply undervalued. There is much work to be done in the world. Sometimes, the people I work with, they do not believe me. They think they cannot do these things. But my determination is enough to make them change their minds."

"They really don't stand a chance," Jex said, his face settled back into careful inscrutability.

Lucía nodded. "I believe it."

"It's not like that!" Amaal objected, but it was

with a laugh. "I simply help match the work and the people. Sometimes I mainstream them into the conventional workforce. Sometimes I help them find a way with their Basic support. I believe anyone can make their way. And when they do, I feel something special in my heart. We all should be self-made, yes? The only question is what self you are making."

Lucía found herself nodding. She couldn't see anyone disagreeing with Amaal's plan for their life, whatever it was. She snuck a look at Jex, who just shrugged like *This is what it is.*

Amaal's gaze quickly swept the room. "Wicket has used his magic on little Eva, didn't he? Before he gets back, and we have our cozy time, I need to finish some business." And with that, she turned, found a straight-backed chair pushed up against the wall, and took a seat. Her eyes glazed as if Lucía and Jex had disappeared from the room. She swiped the air, bringing up a keyboard only she could see, then madly started the fluttering of fingers that meant she was typing. *Down to business.* Lucía was already smitten.

"Well." Jex glanced at the door Amaal had come through. Just then, a soft pattering of footsteps down the stairs announced Wicket's return, sans baby Eva and her mother.

"Lights are back!" Wicket proclaimed.

Jex scowled. "We're still on backup, and I don't know for how long. While I go check, can you introduce Lucía and Joe?" He barely waited for a nod from Wicket before hurrying toward the back door.

"I guess you've met Amaal." Wicket lifted an eyebrow in her direction, but she was absorbed in her display, so he urged Lucía over to the man in the goggles by the front windows, still motionless in his chair. *Joe.* She'd almost forgotten he was there. Wicket tapped the air and flicked toward him, then looked expectant as they eased closer.

Joe winced. "Coming, Wicket," he muttered, then took a deep breath and sighed out the words, "Stories all the way down."

Lucía glanced at Wicket, but he'd just cocked his head to the side, looking impatient.

Joe lifted his googles, squinting at the sudden light. "Sorry, must have missed the alert—" His eyes widened as he saw her. "Oh. Wow." He took out his mute plugs.

Wow?

"Joe, this is Lucía," Wicket said with a look like Joe was being impossible. "Remember, I said she would be here."

"Right. Of course." Joe was marveling at her like he'd never seen a human being before.

"Okay, stop *cataloging* her—you'll drive her off before we even have a chance to show her the rest of us are normal." Wicket gritted his teeth, dramatically, then explained, "Joe is a *writer*. You'll have to excuse him."

"Will I?" She was more amused than annoyed.

Joe lifted his eyebrows as if to say, *Will you?* and continued checking her out.

Wicket sighed. "Jex found him at *The Birdcage* and brought him home, but Joe is hopelessly straight. He also lurks around muscle beach but doesn't lift. There's no explaining it."

Joe rose from his chair, sudden but with a fluid motion like he was waiting for just this moment. "There's always an explanation." Then he looked her dead in the eyes. "Just depends which one you'll believe."

Lucía couldn't tell if he was being deeply flirtatious or just... *strange*.

"Honestly, why do we keep you around?" Wicket asked, although it seemed rhetorical as he peeked over his shoulder at Amaal, still heavily involved in her messaging.

"Probably the Basic support I contribute toward

rent." Joe's smile was teasing but aimed at Wicket, as if Lucía were already in on his joke.

"Do you use Basic, then, to support your writing?" she asked. Everyone got the payments unless you were exempted out—it wasn't a lot, but she'd seen people live off it when they couldn't find work. Or if they did unpaid care with children or the elderly.

Joe folded his arms across his chest. "I'm *employed* at the Birdcage, not a customer, which Wicket conveniently forgot to mention." He tipped his head to her. "Not that it pays much. So, the true answer to your question is *yes,* Basic supports my writing, although mostly it allows me to be *here.* And how lucky for me. What do you do with your time, Ms. Lucía?" He was cataloging her again, this time just her face.

"Ms. Ramirez." She could easily picture a puertorriqueña heroine showing up in one of his stories soon. "I'll be working on Power Island One, starting the day after tomorrow."

Joe's eyebrows lifted. "A genuine hero is among us."

The rest of their banter had just been silly, but that brought a flush to her face. "I'm not, I'm just—"

"I know, right?" Wicket enthused. "Maybe she can help us with the outage."

A flash of uncertainty crossed Joe's face. "You mean the..." Then he glanced over his shoulder at the street outside with the still-darkened street lamps. "Oh." When he turned back, his eyes had narrowed, intense, and focused on her. The floor lamp bulbs reflected off the blue-green of his eyes, making them into tiny interrogation lights. "Yes, our new power engineer ought to be able to explain the outages."

"I don't really..." She stalled out as Wicket's attention zoomed in on her, too. Amaal muttered something to herself, but it was clear she was done and rising up to join them. All eyes were on her. She cleared her throat. "How often do they happen?"

"Once or twice a week." Joe's gaze was even more intense.

"And you don't get any alerts?" That was bad enough, but worse, this was obviously *unscheduled.* She'd checked before setting up her visit, so it wasn't just an alert failure.

"You haven't heard anything about them?" Joe pressed.

"No." But that was a lie. She'd heard *rumors,* but she'd always dismissed them. Power was tightly regulated. People depended on it. The multiple, redundant systems in place, all the backups, the alerts... all of it was designed to precisely avoid this. How could it be happening regularly without everyone on the Islands, not to mention the mainland, being in a complete outrage about it? "I haven't heard anything like this."

"Now isn't that interesting." Joe lifted an eyebrow to Wicket, but he was looking distressed.

"Lucía just came down from Oregon," he sputtered in her defense. "Why would she know anything about what's going on in So Cal?"

But that wasn't an excuse. She *should* know.

"Maybe it's the wildfires," Amaal offered up, now drawn into their circle. "They're earlier every year. It's only June, and look where we are—two million acres?" She was offering Lucía a lifeline as well.

She shouldn't need one. "I can look into it." The promise was out before she thought about what she was saying. "Maybe it's a... an error. In the scheduling." That was the only thing that made any sense. But how could that even happen? Grid balancing was a dark AI art, but someone was monitoring it. How could they not notice? Or maybe someone did, but they were ignored? In any event, this was wrong—and no one should have to tolerate it, certainly not her new family. If they would even have her now.

"An error would be a decent story," Joe said, but not like he was impressed.

"Look!" Amaal pointed to the street. "Power's back."

Lucía peered around Joe—the streetlamps were on.

Joe slid the blocker goggles off his forehead and finger-combed his long-ish hair back into place. Then he dipped his head and said quietly to her, "Just like it never happened." His smirk was irritating, but mostly because it was cryptic. Was he teasing her? Or softening the implied sting of the words?

She frowned. She'd track down whatever this was.

Jex strode through the kitchen door. "Breaker says the power's on. Backups are charging again." He gave Amaal a nod. "They were half power like you said. No idea why."

"Maybe I could take a look," Lucía offered again. Only this time, she knew a lot more about what she might be looking for.

"No!" Wicket spread his hands wide. "Cozy time, *first*. Then you can use your magic power skills on the backups."

Jex seemed perturbed, but Lucía couldn't decide about what or directed at whom. He said nothing, just shook his head and returned to the kitchen.

A touch on Lucía's elbow made her turn. Joe swept his hand away, beckoning her to sit in his upholstered chair while he grabbed a stiff-backed one for himself. "Make yourself comfy," he said with a smile that wasn't so smirky. "You're about to experience Cozy Time with Wicket."

But it was Jex who re-emerged from the kitchen with a tray full of pastries that were tiny works of art —colorful glaze-draped fruits filling thin tart cups. As he passed those around, Amaal brought her chair over to sit by Lucía and Joe, while Wicket planted himself on another seat in the middle of the room. Once Jex had distributed the treats, he settled on the couch against the wall.

"All right!" Wicket literally clapped his hands. "Since Lucía is here, and brand new, we're going to start with a new game Jex made for his channel. It's called *Where's the Lie?* You pull the lie from the deck, and you have to share three truths that are just close enough that we can't tell the difference. Winner gets to skip chores for a week."

Lucía leaned over to Joe. "Is he kidding?"

Joe's smirk returned. "Not in the slightest."

Okay, *games* were not what she expected the first night of her probationary time with a new family. Especially not potentially embarrassing ones. But she hadn't expected an unplanned power outage or homemade empanadillas either. And it turned out, the game wasn't half bad—Jex was a poker-faced demon who would obviously win; Amaal had done so many outrageous things, the lie was always tame by comparison; and Joe's smiles grew less smirky and more warm as the game wore on. Wicket was in his element, and Maria joined them for a second round. Just as cozy time was declared officially over, a young man named Yoram came hurtling in, desperately begging forgiveness, which he did not get from Wicket despite everyone else saying it was fine. Yoram had been at a lab which ran late—he was a student at the same Institute in LA where she had gone to school. Lucía barely got to say hello before Jex rushed him off to do chores, the penance that apparently befell those who violated cozy time's mandatory attendance.

Through all of it, there was a growing ache in her chest. She rubbed at the spot, just below her collar bones, but it was deep inside. It caught Joe's frown, so she stopped. There was no explaining it— everyone was sweet, there was plenty of food. In a short two hours, it was as if she'd known Wicket forever, Amaal was her new favorite human, and Joe and Maria had adopted her as the third leg of their flirtation triad. It was all perfectly wonderful. Later, when Lucía turned in for the night, street lights blazing steadily outside, she finally recognized the persistent, growing soreness in her chest.

Fear. The more perfect the fairy tale, the more harrowing the pain would be when the hit came. And this time, her bedrock would truly crumble into the sea. She could feel it. Her mind might be determined to make it work, and her heart might lift with every smile, but her body remembered—nothing was permanent.

Nothing *stayed.*

That same spot in her chest hurt for a year after her family died. So many were lost during that time. Everyone had a hole punched in them, so she didn't feel particularly alone, especially in Puerto Rico, another island battered by the world. Everyone huddled into each other's arms and held tight. Every shop and street corner had someone's tía looking out for you.

Maybe it was a mistake to leave. But she couldn't know that until she'd tried—and now she needed to give this familia a true shot. And for that, she couldn't build a fortress to keep out the hits. She had to take the risk, out there on the ledge.

Lucía breathed through the ache, like she did so often as a girl, and tried to invite sleep into her mind. She could give it a day. And then she'd be back on the Power Island that was where the dream had first begun.

THREE

THE OCEAN DIDN'T SPEAK, BUT IT DID MUTTER.

Lucía pushed off the rack of turtles and held her breath, cutting the incessant rush of air through the regulator. In that moment of float, even the water sluicing past her body was hushed, leaving her alone with the bubbling white noise of the sea. Every sound carried farther in the water. The towering kelp forests quietly undulated in their reach for the surface sun. Invisible currents jostled the mechanical turtles in their docks. Even Power Island One, floating above and casting its shadow below, sent busy human sounds through the water, fractured and transmuted into a million low tones. The percussion of the sea's voice on her ears was the most soothing thing she knew.

But then she had to breathe. *You're just a visitor down here. Those who forget, drown.*

She settled on the sandy bottom, next to the tower of drones, her own breath now noisy in her ears. It was good to be back in a familiar realm, swaying with the sea, her fins sending up a cloud that swirled around her. The weekend at Jex and Wicket's had gone incredibly well—she'd given the ache in her chest a stern lecture about not dreading terrible things before they happened. If her new family situation fell apart, then it would. Stressing about it now would only make her unreasonable to live with, fulfilling the prophecy of her fears. Besides, imagining heartbreak never stopped it from happening—it only stole the joy from the present.

That was easy to know, harder to believe. But she was determined.

Back to work. She pushed off the sandy seabed and kicked up the tower, rising past the hundreds of docked drones. The TRTL-9000 base model was designed to trawl the kelp forest, checking for health indicators and precisely timing the harvest. The turtles were autonomous, running their own tasks based on the needs of the plants, which were the same bull kelp species she'd tended in Oregon.

She'd uploaded her mods first thing when she'd

arrived on the Island that morning. The drones had been unattended for a week, the previous power engineer having moved on to a new assignment in Australia, so she'd queued up a system check. Her mod synced the turtles with her schedule, so they'd come home to roost just before she dove—simply finding them in their docks was a good sign. She'd spent half her training allotment on her CBT chip and waterproof base station just so she could do this work.

A tap behind her ear to activate, and she was running on thought waves.

Control-by-thought could be dangerous—two hundred feet down was not the best place to have a stray thought scramble whatever you were trying to control—but being touchless had undeniable advantages underwater. The sea's steady thrumming helped her focus as she brought up the menu on the tower's control panel, safe inside its pressurized box. A quick download of the status and malfunction reports to her base station made it faster to skim. Turtle 23 hadn't left its dock in the last cycle, so she swam up the tower to reach it. They were all identical, each a small, boxy suitcase of electronics, along with pincher harvesting arms, micronutrients for ailing kelp, and flippers for locomotion, but this one had snarled up some seaweed in its rotator joint. Now that it was docked, the kelp bulb had jammed up the lock mechanism.

Lucía drew her knife and cut Turtle 23 free. It immediately cycled through its release protocol, and she had to lean out of its path as it wiggled free of its station and headed off, woefully mistiming its mission. She briefly considered sending a reboot signal, but that would require tediously searching the reset codes, and besides, it wouldn't hurt anything.

Before she went back to the logs, she checked her messages. Still no response from her boss, the Island Designer. He had to know something about the unplanned outages on the mainland. Jex's lithium-ion backup wasn't recharging properly, plus he had two more with catastrophic failures. They were older battery tech, but the units were brand new. Her autopsies showed the lithium-titanate nanocrystals on the anode were completely corroded. Some oxidation was normal with each cycle, but not like this. A complete draw-down could have pulled all the lithium ions right out of the material, but that would only happen if the auto cut-off failed. Which a surge might have managed? Then a super-fast, high-voltage discharge could have wiped out the nanocrystals. Maybe. She told Jex there was no fixing it, and he was not pleased about that, but if she had any doubts the outages were not only unplanned but downright weird, the batteries were hard evidence. Whatever was going on, her boss should know, but so far, he was incommunicado.

Lucía might have to physically hunt him down once she was topside, which was an uncomfortable way to meet your boss for the first time. Her reassignment had been handled at the regional level, given the stickiness of her last position. She followed up her earlier message with a meeting request through the Island calendar—maybe that would be sufficient to get him to reply.

Then she pushed off from the tower and slowly floated down while she brought up the reports. CBT was good for complicated tasks requiring fine motor control of the interface, but just swiping through reports was easier to do on manual, so she switched. The display hovered just outside her mask, and she filed each report with a flick of her glove. Most were routine. Harvest requests. Standard reports of rockfish and mollusk populations—everything looked stable. Phytoplankton levels were as important as the kelp in drawing down CO_2 from the atmosphere, but the Islands just monitored those and sent data off to the WSO's marine scientists. She approved the microalgae data and quickly skimmed the rest of the reports. A small herd of sea urchins was encroaching on Sector 15 and eating through the holdfasts—she'd have to send a dedicated turtle team to clear them out. Meanwhile, Turtle 55 had failed to make a report. Sometimes turtles strayed out of range of the docking station and missed a check-in. Her mod should have prevented that, but this happened before the upload. On top of that, Turtle 12 was reporting a diagnostic error and had spent three cycles quarantining itself in its docking station.

Lucía kicked off the sandy floor and swam to Turtle 12's slot first. She cleared out the error and cycled it through a maintenance check, including status on all its appendages and internal supplies... nothing was wrong. And there was no external damage. She cycled it again, but it refused to reset or leave its station. She gave up and sent it a homing command, so it would return to the Island. She'd retrieve it when she was back topside.

That left Turtle 55. Maybe it'd had an unfortunate kelp encounter like Turtle 23. She flutter-kicked up the tower to check it out, but when she reached the docking port... it was gone.

She sighed, as well as one could while using a regulator. She pulled up the turtle's last five reports, plus its movement log. Nothing unusual, and the last known location wasn't far, on the other side of the docking tower, headed toward the—

Why in the world did Turtle 55 go into the shadow?

Lucía peered up. Sunlight filtered unevenly through the kelp, but there was plenty of light for the plants to thrive and to keep the turtles charged. The darkened edge of the five-square-mile floating Island, by contrast, cast a giant no-turtle-land shadow. The drones had limited solar on their backs, with batteries to last them through a cycle, but they all came back to dock for charging. If they wandered off into the shadow, for reasons known only to their autonomous turtle brains, they wouldn't last long. If Turtle 55 went in, it probably ran out of power before it remembered to come back out.

But why go in the first place?

Lucía checked her air. Plenty to track down Turtle 55 and see what mischief it had gotten up to. More importantly, she had an appointment to meet Joe in-game for some immersive he'd invited her to play while she was on the Island. She waited for a school of black rockfish to shimmy past, then kicked her way toward Turtle 55's last synced location. When she crossed into the shadow, the water cooled noticeably. Her thermal suit warmed a little to compensate. She tapped on her headlamp, but the further she swam, the less effective it was in piercing the growing gloom. She unhooked a more powerful dive light from her belt and dove closer to the floor. She hoped Turtle 55 hadn't wandered far enough to reach the vortex rods. But the sandy floor had no sign of dead turtles, and the sound of the rods was growing louder—the chugging of the machinery always sent a chill through her.

Lucía's headlamp swept across the VIV field. *Vortex Induced Vibrations.* She was well-versed in all forms of power, from the fossil-fuel gas-turbines the world still had to use to the miles of wind farms that floated out beyond the Island, but none gave her the same queasy reaction as this giant, churning collection of rods. Rows of them were stacked, one on top of the other, climbing toward the surface like a ladder with moving steps. Hundreds of ladders. The flow of the ocean powered the movement, with the vortices spinning off the rods enhancing the energy. It was bio-mimicry, modeled after schools of fish, each riding in the other's wake. That motion was eventually transformed into electricity via mechanical motors—those were anchored to the concrete floor that had replaced the natural sandy bottom. It was a mechanical wonder, and it was power the world desperately needed, but even the fish knew to keep their distance from this churning nightmare in the dark. It stretched for a mile in each direction, lying directly under the Island and feeding its ocean energy up into the main storage banks.

It was also a giant, ocean-driven, slow-motion blender.

If Turtle 55 had swum into its maw, that was it. Lucía sure wasn't going in after it. The VIV monstrosity rose halfway up to the Island. She hovered before it, her dive light and headlamp illuminating the rods as they churned. The current tugged, drawing her closer. She kicked away, heading up. Would she even be able to see the remains of Turtle 55 in the dark and with all the vortex-blurred water? When she reached the top, she gave the VIV an extra twenty feet of clearance. Then she drifted, slow, turning her dive light up to max power to scan down between the rods, searching for poor Turtle 55. Maybe the vortices had tumbled it to pieces. Maybe it had already been swept away, its remains scattered to the sea.

She was about to give up when she reached a dead spot. She wasn't even sure what she was seeing at first, but all the chaotic motion of the VIV suddenly stilled in one section.

Oh shit, did Turtle 55 break the VIV? Regulators are not conducive to laughing, and Lucía just about drowned herself trying not to. But that settled fast as she peered at the wreckage below, water still churning haplessly into the dead zone. She'd never worked VIVs before, choosing assignments more interesting and less shiver-inducing, but this section was definitely out of commission. She drifted down, a little closer than she really thought smart, right at the center of the dead spot, peering through the blur of her mask and trying to make out the cause of the disaster.

There. In the middle of it. Turtle 55, lying on the artificial ocean floor.

It was sheared in half, but not like it'd been battered by the rods. *Like it had been cut.* Lucía didn't go through years of school without knowing what something looked like when it had been sliced in half by heat. Or maybe electricity. This wasn't stamped or smashed or even ripped apart. Turtle 55 had been split cleanly in half by something with enough power to burn through an autonomous underwater robot. And it wasn't alone. A dozen of the towers of rods had been cut down, lying haphazard as if tossed by a lazy underwater lumberjack.

Whatever had killed Turtle 55 had taken out the VIV.

An alert popped up on her display. She blinked a picture of the carnage and pinned the coordinates then kicked up to a safe distance from the dead spot before she opened the message.

From: Miller Zendek, Designer, Power Island One

To: Lucía Ramirez, Engineer, Power Island One

Lucía, don't get caught up in rumors about outages. People just like to complain. When you've been around a while longer, you'll see how true that is. Welcome to our historic Island! We should have coffee in the garden sometime. Send me an invite.

Lucía read the message twice because *What the hell?* Send him an invite? As if she hadn't just done that? And that swipe about being new, like she was fresh out of the Institute... okay, maybe she didn't have that much experience, but she'd been working on-Island full-time for three years and had plenty of internships before that...

Lucía peered down at the wreckage of the VIV and Turtle 55. She didn't know what was happening here, but it was a hell of a mess. And she had the carcasses of three dead battery packs on the main-land with something to say about that "rumor."

She sent an invite for "coffee in the garden" for the next day. And logged a malfunction report for the VIV, including her snapped picture and coor-dinates.

Guess her first meeting with her boss was going to be uncomfortable after all.

~

FOUR

Lucía strode past the sea lions laid out on the dock, their great blubbery bodies made lazy by the afternoon sun. She'd finished her maintenance check on the solar lilies—they bio-mimicked lily pads, only they were fifty feet across, floating out past the kelp forests that ringed the Island—so it was time to hunt down one Astra Olson, power engineer in charge of the VIV, and woman Lucía needed a word with. Or three. Something like *What the fuck?* but with better phrasing. Or tact, if she could muster it. Astra hadn't replied to Lucía's damage report yesterday *or* her messages today, and that was plain rude.

Lucía pivoted past the string of dinghies, bay boats, and a small research vessel tied up at the dock, then turned inland, taking the most direct route to the office where the Island's locator had placed Astra. The Island was big, five square miles, yet every inch served a purpose. Work and living quarters were spread out—no sense in living on top of each other if you didn't have to—with the rest filled with green tech of one kind or another. In the center loomed a giant, spiraling water tower, visible from every corner. It extended below, bound by tethers to the continental shelf, but the tower mostly served as energy storage. Electric motors pumped seawater up, then that energy was recovered when the water released, flowing down through turbines and back into the sea. It was a giant, but slow, battery—a counter to the massive and much faster flow batteries that stored the Island's power and helped balance the grid. At the tower's base, the desalinator domes formed a ring of smaller latticed structures. In those, a vacuum evaporated the ocean's warm surface water, which was fed into turbines to generate electricity, and finally condensed again by cool water pumped from the ocean's floor. The desal units provided the fresh water for the Island's crops and humans. A dozen other technologies hummed at work, above and below the Island, floating out miles in every direction, even wave and tidal captures closer to shore. It was fair to say the Island was part of a pulsing network of technologies, all tapping the energy the water, wind, and sun offered up, if only engineers like herself could keep the gears running and the ecology in balance to harness it.

Lucía always walked the Island fast—*at Island speed,* a term from her past that no one used anymore —but she couldn't help slowing to watch a ballet of bots in an orchard along the way. It was one of ten gardens that fed the Island's two dozen humans. A weeding bot murderously stamped out a thistle, while a swarm of pollinators lifted from one blossoming pear tree and flitted to the next. The quietly automated reality of this Island was the same as every other she'd seen during school and work... and nothing like what she remembered from her childhood days.

Power Island One.

Her first memories were here. She was only three when she stepped off the boat, clutching Ollie in one hand and her mother's coat in the other. Back then, it was just Energy Island because there was only one, and it hadn't yet started to power the world. The Island then was still experimental, and it pulsed with gigawatts of energy innovation. The race for fusion was still as hot as the plasma they were working to contain. New ideas for renewables, ways to tap the sun and wind and ocean, came fast and furious. It was 2028, and the third climate plague in two years had the world on its heels. The refugee waves had begun, and it must have felt like the world was coming undone—so much it spurred a historic, worldwide collaboration. Some thought renewables were the answer, while others were desperate for fusion to finally have its chance. Energy Island was born as a compromise: off-shore, international waters, funded by every nation and pledged as a shared resource. It was bigger than the Manhattan Project, accelerating every clean energy technology imaginable—and many mostly wishful thinking—including a rush to demonstrate a scalable, net-energy-positive fusion reactor. Hundreds of the world's brightest scientists and engineers lived and worked here, including her parents. They raced to save humanity from the consequences of its own folly and its stubborn unwillingness to change, even as the climate did.

To Lucía, each day had been shiny and exciting and new. Children were few on the Island. She and her two older brothers, Carlos, and Mateo, had run of the place. Technically, there was school, but everyone was busy saving the world—who had time to argue when you wanted to spend your day studying sea lion behavior on the docks? Or hand-carrying lunch to a team of Nobel-prize-winning scientists? Her off-Island teachers were forever forgiving her late assignments, especially when she told them about her secret lab adventures, while the rest of the world had to be content with watching the Island's progress on its official channel. Lucía mostly followed her brothers around, helping with whatever experiments they talked their way into. She could name all the stages of the carbon cycle before she lost her first baby tooth. She became the youngest diver on the Island by age eight. She didn't exactly have friends other than Ollie, but the entire Island was her family.

Until they weren't.

Until the plague took everything and tossed it into the sea.

Lucía blinked, tore her gaze from the mesmerizing dance of the garden bots, then resumed her determined stride along the concrete path. The walkway, the gardens, the bots... none of it was the same. The Energy Island of her childhood didn't exist anymore. It had continued on without her, transforming into something new, while her eight-year-old memories never changed. Her family never left the Island. She met her Tío Luis for the first time at the airport in LA, with just her backpack in hand. He flew her to Puerto Rico. Her familia there welcomed her with kisses and empanadillas. The memory was as clear as the pictures in her private folder. Light captured and stored, on the net and in her brain, only the memories came with feelings. Hard, forever feelings, like you've been kicked out of paradise, but you've still got the photo album. Only she'd done nothing wrong. She was *supposed* to eat from the Tree of Knowledge—her papa had taught her that— but she was kicked out all the same. The virus that took her family was no one's fault and everyone's. And everyone shared the grief that rippled across the world in a wave that nearly swept her away. That's when the memories became her rock, the dream she would keep trying to return to, her Paradise Lost.

When Lucía arrived at the coordinates her locator was tracking, her heart was pounding like she'd run the perimeter of the Island. She stopped to catch her breath, shielding her eyes against the glittering building that supposedly held Astra's office.

This she recognized. It was Dr. Ellis's building. The solar glass coating was new, but it was the same two-story box where she'd spent years pretending to be a very junior assistant to Ellis's fusion team. She couldn't picture the scientist himself, if she'd ever met him at all, but she knew exactly the layout of the entranceway, the wide twin staircase made of marble, and the rooftop garden where she played when she was supposed to be studying.

After she'd left the Island, she'd watched from afar as their experimental fusion reactors failed to produce enough energy to power a Tesla, much less the electricity-hungry city of LA. She was fourteen when the Battery Breakthrough came—new, cheaper flow battery technology that could be built at scale, as well as a range of more exotic systems like magnetic energy storage, along with pumped hydro and other conventional methods. Suddenly, renewable energy could be *stored* on a vast scale. It was the key to moving the needle on decarbonization... and the death knell for fusion. It simply hadn't delivered on all those promises fast enough.

By the time Lucía had her quinceanera—wherein Tito forever earned her love with an ocean-blue taffeta dress—the Island had shut down all the fusion labs. The floating research hub was towed back into US waters and transformed into Power Island One, now piping thousands of gigawatts of clean energy through underwater cables to the mainland. It was replicated all up and down the coast and across the planet. All the innovations of those years matured into a system that could power 80% of the world's energy needs. Not 100% renewables, not yet. And the damage to the planet had been wrought—the world was still under siege, still paying the price of stubbornness, but that was why Lucía was here. Why she followed in her parents' footsteps, trying to claw the world back from the brink of disaster. There was too much loss to stop fighting now.

One step inside showed the building had been transformed just like the rest of the Island. What used to be a bustling research center was now a greenhouse, complete with attendant bots sniffing leaves and poking soil to maintain optimal growing conditions. A large sign over the elevator declared the *Museum of Fusion Technology* was contained within. She vaguely remembered it led to the labyrinth of basement laboratories where the fusion containment systems were housed, down below the surface partly to get access to the extensive water requirements and partly to keep curious eight-year-olds safely away. She knew now the risk would have been minimal. The whole point of fusion—other than the elusive promise of "free" energy—was the inherent safety. Well, as much as you could have with a plasma six times hotter than the sun. The trouble was keeping it hot, not that it would burn everything down. Although it never was as "clean" as the proponents argued—the reactor itself absorbed neutron radiation and became low-key hazardous after a while, plus it contaminated the shielding all around it. Probably not something you wanted an eight-year-old poking around after all.

The tug of curiosity almost had her checking it out—it was a *museum,* after all, one that maybe preserved a bit of her childhood—but she had a schedule to keep.

Lucía found Astra's office on the second floor, the door closed.

She knocked. Waited. Was about to knock again when the door yanked open, but only partially, just enough for Astra's face and body to fill the gap.

"Yes?" It was a demand more than a question, and Astra seemed so startled and almost... *fearful?...* it vaporized Lucía's annoyance.

"Hi, um, I'm Lucía—"

"I know who you are." Astra eased the door open slightly more. She was mid-40's and pale in every way—white-blond hair, pale skin, watery eyes like blue ice. Her eyebrows were so white they disappeared against her skin. Her white lab coat was a strange thing to wear in an office, though. Unless this was a lab? Astra was definitely not inviting Lucía in to find out. "What can I help you with?" Her tone said to make it short.

"I'm sorry if I interrupted..."

Astra narrowed the opening, wedging herself into it as if determined to block Lucía with her body, if required.

What the fuck? applied to the entire woman, not just her message etiquette.

"I wanted to make sure you saw my report on the VIV." Lucía cooled her tone to *I'm here on legitimate business, so deal with me, and then I'll go away.* "It must be cutting into your performance targets—"

"It's fine."

"I mean, it's *not* fine—"

"I don't know what you think you saw." One of Astra's invisible eyebrows popped into existence as she raised it and wrinkled her brow, rendering it as a crease in her face. "But there's nothing on the power logs, no record of damage from the maintenance bots. There's nothing like what you described down there."

Lucía scowled. "Maybe it's been there a while. How far back did you check?" But she knew the damage had to be recent—Turtle 55 had met its demise in the last 48 hours.

"The VIV is fine. Don't you have your own work to worry about?" Astra pale pinkish lips pressed into a line.

Alrighty, then. "I just wanted to give you a heads up." She kept her voice flat. "Before I mention it to Miller. I'm meeting with him in the garden."

"Go ahead. Doesn't matter to me. I told you, there's nothing there." Then she closed the door in Lucía's face.

She stood there a moment, blinking. By the time the shock passed and her face heated, she was already turning on her heel to march away. So far, Power Island One was a disaster. Her memories were an unrealistic overlay on the Island—*this building specifically*—and she needed to recalibrate her expectations. It was already turning out the same as Oregon, where she'd expected a warm Island family but found a dozen people scattered across a floating power node, busily attending their own sectors to keep the world running but avoiding each other even in their off-time. *Or not,* as the leering image of her stalker helpfully reminded her.

Were the people of Energy Island really so different back then? There was no way for her to know—she only saw it through the unreliable lens of a child's eyes. Maybe they simply indulged her? Or maybe the work was different now, drawing in the kind of person who thrived when they could be alone. Plus, some people were more at home with bots than humans. She could even understand it, to a certain extent. The solitude was freedom—you could make your own rhythms, craft your daily routines however you liked. No one cared as long as the power stayed on.

Maybe that was it—maybe Astra thought Lucía was barging in, new to the Island and finding fault with the engineers who'd already set up their careers here. Or *maybe* Astra was wildly incompetent and never left her "lab." The Island's automation was so complete, one could get away with a full-time side business of makeup tutorials or a channel devoted entirely to tasting donuts. Not that she subscribed to those.

Ahem. Maybe she shouldn't judge whatever Astra had going on behind her closed door.

Regardless, there was something wrong with the VIV, and while Lucía didn't want to cause trouble for a fellow engineer, she *had* given Astra a chance to address it. No one could blame her for taking this to the designer.

Her trek across the Island, under the shadow of the water tower and around the desal domes, gave her time to get her head straight. She paused at a long hedge of raspberry bushes and stole a snack off a branch between passes of a harvesting bot. She was new to the Island. She'd reported the damage. She could be forgiven if that was a breach of unspoken protocol. This coffee with Miller should get that straightened out. If necessary, she could take a hit on that as a learning experience about the Island's culture, make her *mea culpas*, and stay out of everyone's way for a while. She wanted this to work—she wanted more game time with Joe, more cozy time with Wicket—and that meant keeping her job for more than a day.

With that resolve, she marched on to the garden. This one had knee-high corn, tomatoes, spinach, and a host of other veggies on rotation that would show up in their meal deliveries—or get exported to the mainland. The limited human staff on-Island included a chef who commanded an army of harvest bots. There was no eating like Island eating. This garden had made a virtue of the bot tending paths to form a short maze to the gazebo in the center. The small table-for-two was already occupied by one Miller Zendek, two earthen mugs of coffee, and a pair of tiny paper bowls of creamer dots and sugar cubes. A hospitality bot sat in the shadow of one corner of the gazebo, powered down.

Miller rose as she trotted up the three steps. He smiled in a way that felt colder than it looked. "Welcome to Power Island One, Ms. Ramirez!" He bowed quickly, the proper formal greeting for business, but he didn't drop his gaze like you normally would, keeping a keen eye on her. She stopped a few feet away to return the bow, gaze properly dropped, arms at her side.

When she looked up, his cold smile had settled into a smirk.

"It's good to be here," she said, still standing, awkward, a few feet from the table.

"Again. Right?" He gestured for her to sit.

She frowned. "Um. I guess?" She took the few steps to finally reach the middle of the gazebo, and they sat together.

"I believe you were on the Island before *me*."

"Oh. Yes." She'd read his profile—the *wunderkind* designer who'd transformed Energy Island into Power Island One, overseeing the design of literally all the other Islands. He was mid-thirties but already had done more in his career than she would probably ever do in hers. "I was just a kid then."

"Ah, your parents would be proud to see you here now." He beamed like he had been authorized to hand out compliments on behalf of her dead parents and had judged her, marginally, worthwhile.

It was so strange, she wasn't sure what to say. "I'd like to think so."

"Do you take sugar?" Miller lifted his chin to the coffee set.

"I like to keep things simple." Which was the best segue she could manage. "About the VIV report—"

He cut her off with a wave. "We'll get to that. But first..." He picked up his mug and held it out. "A toast to your return to your home Island. May you build nothing but pleasant memories from this moment forward."

She almost missed the clinking of mugs Miller was after. But she managed, choking out, "Thank you," before sipping her coffee. It was bitter and cold.

"It's a shame I came to the Island after your parents had already passed."

She just blinked. He obviously had something to say, so she'd just let him say it.

"Otherwise, I might have gotten to know them," he continued. "Miranda Ramirez was truly an exceptional marine biologist. I see you're following in her footsteps with your focus on the aquatic features of the Island."

He'd read her records. Of course, he had—but why was he making such a deal out of it? "I'm fully trained in all power engineering systems, even tech that's mostly on the mainland."

"Yes, of course, you are." He smiled again. It had an unfulfilled ambition to be warm. "Let me be straight, Ms. Ramirez. I've worked hard to build a network of Power Islands the country can depend upon to power their lives—sustainably and in a way that will help fight the climate crisis. And while I want every Power Island to be efficient and well-run, Power Island One is the original. The premier. I don't have to tell you the historical significance of this floating piece of community property off the Southern California coast." He was leaning back in his chair now, easing into the words like he was used to a captive audience. "It's not that we never have problems here—we're not immune to the occasional glitch, just like anywhere else—but we needn't go looking for problems that don't exist."

She'd been trying to sociably nurse her coffee,

but she gave that up and set it down. "I'm not sure I take your meaning." But a rush of cold was settling in her stomach. Was he firing her already? Could he even *do* that? There were job protections, after all, especially for power workers. And she had done nothing wrong.

"I mean..." He leaned forward, folding his hands on the table and cocking his head, almost as if he was pitying her. "I'm sure you saw *something* down at the VIV, Lucía. Maybe a pod of dolphins playing and kicking up sand."

What? "I filed an image of the damage." Literally no one could look at that and think *dolphins*—not unless marine mammals had acquired massively powerful underwater cutting technology when she wasn't looking.

Miller frowned. "Are you sure?" He leaned back again, gesturing with an open hand. "I examined your report. There were no images attached."

She stared at him for a beat. "No images."

He shrugged. "None that I could find."

She quickly flicked a look to the side, activating her display, then tapped her CBT on to thought-control a search to bring up her report.

"You can look if you'd like," Miller was saying, with a smile because he obviously knew she was checking. "The point is, I'm sure it's a simple mistake. You saw something. Your imagination ran away with you. And, perhaps being an eager new employee on our historic Island, you wanted to make an impression."

"I didn't..." She stopped as the report came up. *No image.* She flipped through her standard image storage, backups of everything she'd ever blinked... *nothing.* As if she'd never taken the picture. It wasn't impossible for her chip capture to have glitched out, but... "I could have sworn..." She tore her focus from her display back to Miller's pitying expression. "I don't know what happened to the picture, but I saw it. The rods were *cut.*"

"I'm sure you saw something." His smile grew. "It's all right. Astra assures me that everything's in order with the VIV, so you needn't worry about it. And while we're on the subject of things you don't have to worry about... the outage you mentioned, on the mainland. Did that affect your family?"

The whiplash change in subject made her chest squeeze. "I was there when it happened."

His pitying look took on a new intensity. Like he was beginning to worry about her mental health. "Glitches definitely happen on the grid. The AI is always optimizing usage, and there is occasionally some small unintended result that emerges from that optimization. We don't like to talk about it, but it very rarely does happen. Send me the coordinates of your new family, and I will *personally* look into it and make sure nothing inconveniences them again." He smiled and waited.

Her heart lurched, but what choice did she have? She manually swiped open her address book and sent the coordinates to Miller. Then she dropped her hand to her lap before it could shake. A flick of his attention said he'd received it.

"Now that that's taken care of..." He rose up, smoothly but so unexpectedly that Lucía was left to lurch to her feet. "I have a packed calendar this afternoon, which I really should get back to. It was delightful to meet you, Ms. Ramirez. I hope you'll get settled into our beautiful Island soon." He didn't bother with bowing this time, just turned and strode away, back straight, off to do the important work that an Island Designer of his stature no doubt engaged in every day.

She stood watching him until the hospitality bot woke itself up and came to clear the coffee. Then she hustled out of the gazebo, taking the opposite path out of the garden maze from Miller, just to make sure they didn't cross paths... and headed straight for the docks.

Turtle 12 was still sitting in the rehab bin where she'd stashed it earlier. She pulled it out, lugging the forty-pound suitcase of electronics to the dockside shop. The turtle was much heavier on land, plus completely unable to self-propel outside the water. She ran another system check, and that cleared out whatever hiccup Turtle 12 had about leaving its dock. Then she did a physical exam to make sure nothing else was wrong, triple checking the camera. Last, she uploaded a new mission script along with the coordinates from the damage report on the VIV. With a flipper check to make sure it was ready for action, Lucía hauled it back to the dock and, with a practiced *heave,* tossed Turtle 12 into the water.

It wouldn't take long for it to reach the VIV.

The sun was getting lower in the sky. Her meal would be delivered to her room soon. She strode across the Island, heading "home" but keeping a visual monitor of Turtle 12's onboard camera up on her display. Just as she reached her apartment—a renovated shed near the desal units—Turtle 12's mission log reported it had reached the coordinates.

The VIV churned in the turtle's spotlight.

There was no sign of damage. Just vortices of

water shedding off the churning rods and producing power for the VIV.

"What the hell." Her voice was a whisper even though there was no one nearby to hear.

Whatever she'd seen was gone now.

Including Turtle 55.

FIVE

Lucía's "home" on the Island was a garden shack.

When she'd arrived yesterday morning, she'd looked for her family's apartment, but it was gone. The shack belonged to the previous power engineer, the one whose duties she'd taken over. They'd transformed it into a tiny home that felt like it was underwater. One wall was a single display that stretched between the main room and the bathroom. Lucía left it on the time-delayed Great Barrier Reef cam. The previous owner had clearly gotten their dream job down under. Power Islands were involved in a lot of restoration work, and that plus expansive no-fish zones were helping the reefs make a comeback. She didn't have to imagine how beautiful it was—her entire living space was one long reef dive. And while that, and the turtle shower knobs and the sailboat-themed everything was fun, there wasn't much room to pace.

And the agitation in Lucía's body was working up to a full riot.

She saw what she saw on the VIV. *Or did she?*

Was she losing her mind?

She sat down on the edge of the ocean-blue bed that took up most of the single-room apartment and opened a work pad on her display. Sketching manually, she drew the damaged VIV from memory. Then she added a hapless and bisected Turtle 55 lying in the middle. From that and some specs on the VIV rods she pulled up from the Island's database of materials, she calculated how much energy would be required to cause the damage she saw. It was substantial, but not impossible. More than your standard welding torch, but a large enough underwater laser or half a dozen other cutting technologies for salvage could do it. *Why* someone would want to sabotage the VIV, she had no idea. But putting it back together?

She checked the timestamp on her report—twenty-nine hours and fifteen minutes ago. And half of that in the dark, although the VIV was in Island shadow anyway. If someone started the minute she was back topside, somehow had VIV parts lying around, shut down the whole thing, got in there and welded, repaired, and cleaned up... it would take a small army of bots, many of which would have to be reprogrammed for job-specific tasks, including a larger plan to map out the repair, plus several technician-divers and all kinds of support equipment... even so, any reasonable operation would take a couple days. She checked the VIV operational logs. No record of it being shut down *at all,* and it generated a non-trivial amount of power—that level of loss wouldn't go unnoticed, much less undocumented.

She swiped it all away and stood up.

It was crazy. Maybe not impossible, but it made no damn sense.

She paced the five steps to the front door and back again. Then she opened a message channel to Joe. *I think I've lost my mind.*

His reply came back fast—he was probably in immersive, using his CBT. *I'll assemble a search party immediately.*

She smiled. *Are you in the middle of something?*

Nothing I can't gleefully abandon for a side quest to find Lucía's mind. That's far too precious a thing to lose.

That gave her a warm flush. *I could join you in-game.*

I'm already back at my virtual base. Here's an invite. An envelope danced in the corner of her display.

Hang on, I have to get my goggles. He'd given her a pair, and mute plugs too, before she'd left for the Island. She hadn't brought much with her, leaving her Ollie-the-octopus and her few personal things at the cottage. A sort-of promise to return.

She swiped the goggles and mute plugs off the end table by the bed, then propped herself up against the pillows, sitting cross-legged, palms upturned, like Joe had taught her. His advanced immersive chip had full-body haptic, motor block, CBT, the works. Hers was CBT-only, but with an optional upgrade for a motor block she'd simply never installed. It was supposedly safe, but triggering sleep paralysis by dosing yourself with neurotransmitters wasn't the kind of thing you wanted to go off accidentally. But for immersive, it was necessary—couldn't have your body trying to leap out of the bed while in-game. Joe insisted she set up a safe word—*Nereocystis,* the genus of bull kelp—to allow her to abort the block and wake up her body if the normal transition out of immersive didn't work. He advised to only game with a partner, in case you got stuck. Seemed reasonable.

She popped in the plugs and settled the goggles over her eyes. With everything dark, all she could see was her display. She brought her CBT online with a tap behind her ear, then thought-opened Joe's invite. A prompt reminded her to activate the block. "I consent to a motor block." The voice print took, and she felt her body go slack a split second before being visually whisked away to Joe's virtual base.

His full haptic implant required a *lot* more filaments in the brain than she was altogether comfortable with, but all the other senses were part of the standard package. Her CBT upgrade made everything pretty intuitive, even without the haptic. Once the disorientation of the transport settled, she was fully immersed in Joe's virtual base.

"Wow," she said. Or thought-said. It came out of her virtual self's mouth, and Joe turned toward her. She was still sorting the terminology. But the place was amazing—brightly lit with artificial sun, as cozy as anything off Jex's *Easy Pleaser* channel, with over-stuffed chairs and couches heaped with pillows.

"Hey, you got here fast." His avatar looked just like him, only with less of a shave and a t-shirt that said *Reality is just an illusion.* "And... this is the inside of my head. Sorry, it's a mess."

But it wasn't a mess—it was a tidy room lined with shelves holding paper books. A half dozen lay open with crisp white pages and neat black lettering, while a dozen more stood in small stacks on the couch, chair, and floor. "Do you actually read these?" she asked, thought-moving to the chair and reaching for one. Physics was weird in-game, or at least in-immersive and without haptic—there was no physical feedback to train up your brain. It took a little getting used to, but she was already better than yesterday's stumbling dragon hunt.

"I know it's shocking," Joe said, his avatar striding smoothly up next to her, no sudden teleportation like she had to use, "but writers tend to actually read books. It's a way to sneak up on the words and catch them before they can scurry away."

She was still trying to pick up the book, finally getting it on the third try. There was no sensation, of course, but she managed to flip through a couple pages then turned it to look at the cover. "'Do Not Stand at My Grave'?"

"Irish Death Poetry." His cringe was very realistic in virtual. "You wouldn't be interested." He took the book from her, closed it up, and tucked it under his arm. "So, what's this about losing your mind? You seem remarkably intact for a mindless golem. Although still smartly dressed for dragon slaying, I see." He swept a look over her.

She peered down. Her avatar was still decked out in the layered leather armor she'd chosen for their game yesterday. He'd helped craft it—she could have been anything but opted to do a facial scan that reproduced her features and matched her exact medium-brown skin tone. "I don't know how to change."

"And I'll be the last to ask you to." He was flirting with her again—really, always—and she didn't exactly mind, but she had messaged him with a purpose.

"Remember the VIV I told you was broken? That I filed the report for? It's not."

"How do you mean?" He frowned and placed the book on a short stack on the couch. "I thought you said your turtle and the VIV were both slaughtered in some kind of underwater massacre."

"They were. But then Miller said they weren't. And he was right."

Joe's frown deepened. "He's your boss, right?"

Lucía nodded—well, she meant to nod. She wasn't sure if Joe could see it. "Yes, he's my boss and kind of an asshole. I'm off to a terrific start with both him and Astra, the engineer in charge of the VIV. They both think I'm *confused.* That I didn't see what I saw. And now it's just gone. *Fixed.* Only it's crazy that it could have been fixed that fast. It's like it never happened."

"Wait, didn't you blink a picture?"

"That's gone, too."

Joe's eyebrows lifted, and his mouth formed an *oh.* Then he scowled and scooped books off the couch, making a spot for her. Yesterday, she'd mastered thought-moving upright and five ways to swing a sword, but sitting hadn't been required. She willed herself to the edge of the cushion then thought about how it would feel to sit down. She did... then promptly slid off and ended up on the floor.

"Shit." She wasn't even sure how to get back up, so she just stayed and covered her face with her hands.

"Okay, come on," Joe said, "we can sort this out." He lifted her hands away from her face, and somehow, he'd moved her up onto the couch.

"I suck so bad at this." She meant the immersive, but it could equally apply to making allies on the Island. It was just like Oregon all over again, which would make her stomach clench if she actually had a stomach that could clench and not a virtual body. So weird. How did people get addicted to this? It all felt unnatural to her.

Joe dipped his head and lifted his eyebrows, a cute flirty look. She had no idea how he managed it. "You're better than my grandma."

She laughed, at least in her head. Her avatar kind of made a sound too. "You really shouldn't flatter me so much."

He pulled a look like he was affronted. "Hey, my grandma rocks!" Then he spun his hand in the air, and a mug of steaming coffee appeared in it. She could tell by the *smell,* which captured her attention completely. He gave it to her, then spawned in his own. Hers tasted like the best dark roast she'd ever had.

"Amazing." She took another sip. Okay, she might understand the attraction. "Why do you even bother with real coffee?"

"That is an excellent question." He rested his mug on the couch between them and leaned closer. "The kind a perceptive, intelligent woman asks. The sort of woman who is *not* confused about broken power equipment she sees underwater."

"But I am—I don't even know what to think about this."

"Miller's obviously gaslighting you. Astra's probably lying to cover up something she did. The question is *why?* What the hell did you see down there? And why go to all this trouble to make you *unsee* it?"

She took another sip of the coffee, holding it close to her face with both hands just because that was easier than figuring out how to set it down. "You don't think I'm crazy?"

Joe smiled broadly. "You're the least crazy person I know. It's utterly charming."

She shook her head and smiled, then sipped more coffee and thought about it a moment. If she wasn't hallucinating—if Turtle 55 really was sliced up and now was swept up in some grand conspiracy to cover up damage to the VIV—what was she going to do? What *could* she do?

"Miller wants me to forget all about this."

"Fuck that guy."

She laughed. "Well, he's my boss. Probably not a recommended solution."

Joe's face contorted in disgust. "Not *at all* what I meant."

With great concentration, Lucía set the mug on the couch between them. The mug didn't exist. The couch didn't exist either. And yet, it was extremely difficult to get one to sit on top of the other without tipping or banging into Joe's mug. Even harder to move her hands, so they simply lay in her lap, staying out of trouble. It wasn't like she hadn't done virtual before, but immersive was different. No controllers. All CBT. And for her, no haptic to guide her.

She looked into Joe's eyes. Also not real. And yet the micro-expressions of his face were so detailed, her mind just filled in the rest. He wasn't Joe's avatar —*he was Joe.* And a friend. Maybe more, but not yet. It had that dangerous feeling, same as when she was welcomed into Jex and Wicket's fairy-tale house back on the mainland, where Joe's body actually sat, probably in the front room next to the windows. The nicer this felt—the flirtation, the friendship and support—the more it would hurt later when it got ripped away. Or she was forced to leave. Or they kicked her out.

Don't imagine the heartbreak before it happens, her better side scolded her.

But if she was going to risk all that, *again,* she might as well do it completely. "I grew up here, on the Island. Until I was eight, anyway, and my family died. It was ATP-34, Arctic Thaw Paleovirus. My immune system fought it off. Then I went back to Puerto Rico."

"Oh, *shit*... Lucía... I'm sorry." He leaned back a little. "This is like your home. No, it *is* your home. Literally. Is this your first time back?"

She smiled a little. "Yeah. It's really nothing like I remember. And that's just it. I keep chasing this... *dream*... as if I can recapture that time, back when things were good, and it just never works out. I wanted to be a power engineer, so I could return to the Islands. Then Oregon was a mess..." She trailed off, not wanting to go into all that.

"You had a stalker," Joe prompted. "Jex told me."

The tension she was holding—and it had to be mental because there wasn't anything else in immersive—released. "Except no one believed me. I told Jex that my co-workers didn't have my back, and that's why I left, but it was more than that. The family I was part of—I'd been with them for *years,* two of those formally adopted—they didn't believe me, either. Only, they kind of did. It was this weird combination of saying I was lying, yet also they didn't want me bringing trouble into their home."

"*Their* home." Joe got it. Instantly.

"Yeah." But her relief was having a cage fight with her fear. She had to look away, dropping her gaze to the two mugs of coffee still between them. *Be honest, Lucía. He can't help if you shut him out.* "It was so... not what I expected. I kept thinking maybe there was something wrong with me, you know, having all these problems." *Too much,* her head screamed as she peeked up to check his reaction.

"Okay, hold up." Joe was frowning. "There's nothing wrong with you."

"That you *know* of." She forced a smile, but he just scowled more. "I'm off to a *great* start here on the Island, connecting with people." She shook her head because it really was a disaster. "Oregon was a mess. My family up there basically kicked me out. Then I come down here, and already, everything's going wrong?" She realized how that sounded. "On the Island," she rushed out, "not the cottage. I loved this weekend. Really. And I super appreciate you letting me bounce all this off you. I just don't know what this is with the VIV, and I'm pretty sure if I keep pushing, I'll be out of a job. Then I become the problem. They'll probably send me on a six-month tour on a mid-Atlantic Island." Then she'd lose her chance to see if things at the cottage even *could* work out. Or if it truly was her that was broken.

Joe didn't look any happier. "Would you move

back to Puerto Rico instead?" His expression had fallen blank, almost like he didn't want it read.

"I could find work there. My family would love it. But Island work is all I've ever wanted to do. And Puerto Rico's an island, but not a Power Island."

His face became animated again, lit up. "Then you fight for it."

"I'm just *tired,* Joe."

His brow wrinkled up with concern.

"No, that's not really it." She avoided his earnest face, looking around at his virtual base. It was all the things he loved—books, coffee, a cozy place to retreat. His immersive games on tap in a display on the wall. And she'd already seen the fairy-tale house he lived in with Jex and Wicket and the others. *He had the dream.* How could he understand? "I look at this, and you, and Jex and Wicket, and how everyone is with each other..." She faced him again. "I know it's possible. I *remember* that feeling—that you belonged, were safe, everything would turn out all right, even if your turtle wandered off and got you both in a bunch of trouble. I know that kind of home—not the physical kind, but the feeling of it— exists. I just don't know if I'm ever meant to have it again."

"*Lucía.*" He seemed genuinely pained for her.

Not the pity she sometimes saw, but *pain.* It made her look away again.

"I'm not afraid of losing my job," she said to the brightly lit fake windows. They were frosted, the world undefined, non-existent, beyond them, just an infinite soft glow. "I'm not afraid of dying. Not the way other people are. I've seen enough of that. I know it's always there. Death just *is.* It's not up to me when it comes. I'm just afraid..." It took her a long moment to turn back to face him this time. His eyes were wide, not pained, but he was hanging on her words. "I'm afraid I'll live my whole life, however long that is, and the best will have ended when I was eight."

Joe's avatar was struggling for words. It was like he'd retreated inside the avatar mask of himself for a moment, pulling back from her intensity. She should have known better than to just spill out everything. She was all-or-nothing that way. Hold it all back, give nothing away... or take a rib-spreader to her chest and bare her shredded heart. Her family back in Puerto Rico would think nothing of it—everyone was just *out* with what they felt, *passionate,* sometimes too much even for her. But here, on the mainland, she'd quickly figured out it was too much for most.

She winced. "I'm sorry—"

"*No.*" Joe's face transformed into *realness* again. It was amazing to watch it happen, even if she didn't understand the technology behind it. "Don't ever apologize for being that... *open.*" He was still struggling, kind of breathless, even though breathing wasn't a thing you did in immersive, and she just watched, waiting for him to sort whatever it was. Embarrassment? Confusion? Puertorriqueñas like her could be *a lot,* as Tito would say. She never felt like that was true for her, but maybe it was more true than she knew. "Are you not close to your family in Puerto Rico?" Joe asked as if lifting that thought from her head.

"No, I am." She frowned. "I mean, they're my kin. They had to adopt me in, I suppose. And so many families did, not just my Tío Luis and Tía Benita. They absolutely love me. And I love them. It's just..." It was her turn to struggle for the words. "They didn't *choose* me. Not like my parents. I just kind of showed up, washed ashore, and they took me in. It's different than an intentionally chosen family. I guess? I'm not sure what I'm saying. But it's different. Not like it would be now, as an adult, with a new family."

"With us." He blinked. "Jex and Wicket, I mean."

She smiled. "You hardly know me, and here I am dumping all my *everything* on you. Oh, and by the way, I'm bringing my work troubles home again, too." *Home.* The word just slipped out, and she wanted to snatch it back, but it was slippery and loose, out in the immersive already.

"It's fine."

She winced. "No, it's not. And I mean it literally. Miller asked for the coordinates of the cottage. He's going to *personally* look into the outages. What if I've sucked you into this thing, whatever it is? That's not okay. Maybe even worse than what happened in Oregon."

He didn't seem freaked out by that. He picked up both their mugs and made them disappear, clearing the way for him to edge closer on the couch. She wouldn't feel anything if he touched her in immersive—but he would feel it, which made the whole idea asymmetrical and bizarre. Fortunately, that didn't seem to be his plan.

He peered intently into her eyes. "First, don't worry about us. We'll be fine. Second, this is your home Island—and something very weird is going on. I don't think you can walk away from that. Or stay but simply ignore it. However, this isn't something small. And I don't like any of it. Disappearing images? Out of your personal folder? That's a serious breach."

It was a relief to be talking about the VIV again. "That's got me spooked, too."

"You need to be careful. Check it out without letting them know you're checking it out. Maybe it's some petty corruption. Maybe Miller just doesn't want the Island to look bad. Do a little investigating, be careful, and maybe it will turn out to be not much of anything. Then you can stay, do the work you love, and it'll all be fine."

She nodded. That sounded like a plan, at least.

"Here's the most important part, though: I'm with you on this. Okay? We're partners. I don't have any legal papers to sign or formal pledges to offer—I'm just saying I'll have your back as you go through this. And you can come fix our backup power supply whenever you like. Deal?"

She smiled and clumsily offered her hand to shake. It was the kind of thing you did when making important business deals. Which this wasn't, so that made it not so serious. "Deal."

He took her hand, and there was a flash of something in his eyes, but then he smiled and released her. "We'll have a proper handshake when you get back to the mainland. When is that again?"

"Four weeks."

"All right. Plenty of time to break up whatever secret underwater arms deals Miller's conducting."

She laughed, and it almost sounded normal, despite the tech.

The relief was real. She'd told him everything—too much, probably—and he was still here, offering to help. She hadn't scared him off.

Maybe this would work out after all.

SIX

INVESTIGATING.

Lucía was an engineer, not a detective, but solving problems was what she did, and this VIV mystery just required extra creativity. She had full access to the Island's systems, both physical and digital, although whoever wanted to cover up the VIV damage had already shown they could erase records. And not just of the VIV—Turtle 55's logs were gone too as if the bot had never existed. Her private records, in her photo folder... those were supposed to be untouchable. Did Miller hack into her accounts? Did he have enough pull to get clearance from Digital Management Services to erase her records? DMS should require a court order, and she couldn't imagine that happened in a day. Joe was right in what he said yesterday—this *had* to be dirty, so she needed to be careful. Come at it from a different angle.

Which was how she found herself marching to the Museum of Fusion Technology.

After the morning's turtle check—Turtle 55's dock was still empty—she'd done her own visual check of the coordinates where the VIV had been damaged. Not only was everything intact, but the supports for the VIV's churning rods had a solid layer of algae and barnacles. No way that had grown back overnight. Sticking with the assumption she wasn't hallucinating, whoever did this must have swapped the parts out from somewhere else. She searched the nearby VIV for signs of shiny new replacements, but it was huge. Most of the Island shadow was filled with VIV fields. Which was what made her, finally, look *up*—what part of the Island was directly above the previously-damaged VIV?

She had to wait to get topside again to plot it, but it turned out...

The Museum of Fusion Technology.

She stopped at the elevator and flicked a quick look to the stairs. The locator said Astra was in her "office" again. Lucía waved her hand to call the elevator car, then tried not to squirm while she waited. The *ding* of the doors opening just about stopped her heart. She hurried in and pushed the one button. A small plate saying *Museum* had been tack welded over the original designation. She relaxed once the doors slid closed.

The elevator took painfully long to get there. When it opened, it revealed a tiny entranceway to the museum, with a podium standing next to closed double doors. The *James B. Ellis Fusion Museum* was emblazoned above, with a smaller plaque below it that read *The sun is also a star*. Light snuck out from beneath the doors.

Lucía brought up the coordinates for the wrecked VIV, and the direct mapping at this level was yet another fifty feet beyond the doors. When she tried, they were unlocked—she couldn't be accused of breaking in—and the museum was fairly small. The perimeter held displays, videos, and stills of the various incarnations of fusion reactors. A scale model of the original ITER, International Thermonuclear Experimental Reactor, sat in the middle of the room, just the toroid reactor itself, about fifteen feet across, stripped bare of its supporting equipment. She'd never seen one in person and was drawn to the complex and precision-built design, a toroid of plated metal like an armadillo, if all its armor had been turned inside out. ITER was an early generation Tokamak design that used a magnetic field to hold the 150 Million Degree C plasma. Fusion's promise had been as bright as the star it tried to contain. ITER was supposed to achieve First Plasma the year she was born, but tech problems and the climate crisis compounded to delay it. Three years later, amid the escalating pandemics, Energy Island was born, and most major fusion research was moved to the Island at that time. After thirteen years, and almost as many major iterations on the containment design, fusion research was shut down for good, having never fulfilled those starry-eyed promises.

The sound of a door opening behind the reactor yanked her attention away. She froze, briefly considering a run for the elevator, but the scuffling hurry of shoes was too close. A tall, gangly, older man with a shock of white hair emerged from behind the reactor.

"I'm sorry, the museum is closed." His face was flushed like he'd been sprinting to reach her. His eyes narrowed as he quickly took in her standard Island-issued coveralls and nametag. *"Ramirez.* You must be new." He wore the same clothes, no tag.

She finally found her voice. "Sorry, I was just curious." She edged around the reactor, peering at the door he had come from. The room wasn't that deep. The coordinates lay beyond the second door. "Is there more to the museum back there?"

"No." He shifted slightly, subtly blocking her view. "Just storage. If you'd like a tour, I give guided ones every other Friday morning for the school kids. It's on the schedule. You can come back then." He gave a wan smile that seemed like all the effort he could muster.

"So, you're the museum keeper?" She frowned a little, then subtly tapped behind her ear to activate her CBT, thought-commanding up the Island's internal roster. She didn't recall Museum Keeper being an official position on the Island, not that she spent a lot of time checking.

His squint said he knew she was checking. He fished into his pocket and came out with a nametag— looked like it was home printed. *J. Casimir.* "Johannes Casimir," he said. "I'm a volunteer. Actually, a historian. This is my part-time avocation, preserving the history of these artifacts of the coming-of-age of the power industry. I'm not on the payroll if that's what you're checking."

She gave him a tight smile. "Just wondering. I am new, like you say." She flicked a look at the back door again. "So, you're preserving the real fusion reactors?" *Volunteer* was not the kind of thing the Islands had. Even visitors needed special clearance. Was he some kind of crazy enthusiast? Trying to fire up a fusion reactor on his own?

"The equipment was criminally abandoned if you ask me." The indignation in his voice straightened his whole lanky body. His hair had a wildness of its own, sticking out at odd angles, like he'd tried to smooth it down repeatedly, then given up. "One day, these scientists were on a valiant quest to save the world with the most miraculous kind of power—clean, free, powered by the elements of the universe, almost as if it were a gift from the gods themselves—and the next moment, everything was abandoned. Funding was gone, everyone kicked out. They even bolted the doors to keep people from taking some of the equipment with them. *Souvenirs.*" His disgust was full-wattage.

She smiled in spite of herself. "Grave robbers."

"While the body was still warm!" His voice was a growl, but the suspicion in his eyes softened a little. He muttered under his breath, then affixed his non-regulation nametag to his coveralls.

"Casimir?" she asked, giving it another look. Sure, it was homemade, but maybe he really was a volunteer historian. "Like the Casimir effect?" She was no physicist, but it was briefly covered in her quantum mechanics class.

He stopped fussing with the tag and held his chin high. "You are looking at the great-nephew of the man himself, Hendrik Brugt Gerhard Casimir." He waved his hand with a dramatic flourish, and Lucía nearly laughed. Then she remembered she was supposed to be *investigating*.

She narrowed her eyes. "The Casimir effect has to do with small perturbations in a quantum field between two plates. Gives rise to a force at very small distances. Important in nanotechnologies."

"Just so." Johannes gave a slight bow.

"But not exactly fusion tech. What drew you to curate all this old technology?"

"*Old* technology!" He seemed personally offended. "These machines are younger than I am."

She smiled again. "I meant no offense."

He sighed. "Things become obsolete faster and faster every year. We're too *impatient,* that's all. They simply couldn't wait, couldn't invest the necessary time and expertise and commitment to science to give fusion a chance. And now, what do we have? A museum instead of a reactor. *And kelp.* It is not a major scientific achievement to grow a weed in the sea."

She raised an eyebrow. He sounded disgruntled, but then maybe that's what you became when you were an archivist for abandoned tech. "I guess that makes me a gardener."

He harumphed and looked only slightly contrite. "No offense, Ms. Ramirez. The green tech of the Island is very important."

"We do power most of the country," she offered, although surely he knew. She wasn't even offended, mostly amused. "A little more every year."

"Yes. Well. If you don't mind..." He gestured toward the entrance door. "I've left some parts sitting in citric acid. Trying to remove some rust. It's a long and tedious process that must be carefully monitored, and I must return to it."

"Sure." Although, she was certain this was just an excuse. "Every other Friday for the tour?"

"Yes." He'd shuffled her to the door. "Although you should check the schedule. It's summer now, and I don't think we have any students coming for some time." He opened the door but paused, his expression less abrasive. "Perhaps, if you are the only one, I could give a special tour for a more educated student."

She smiled wider. "That would be nice." She slipped out, and he closed the door behind her. On the ride up the elevator, she almost hated the obvious fact that he was hiding something. Maybe it wasn't anything nefarious. He *had* invited her back—surely, he wouldn't have done that if he were secretly firing up ancient fusion reactors in a quest to prove all the naysayers wrong.

But it nagged at her all the way back to her room.

Because if Mr. Casimir *was* firing up the old reactors, maybe there had been an accident. Fusion was notoriously safe—the problem was keeping the reaction from fizzling out—but had he lost containment in a spectacular way, well, a hundred million degrees is a lot of energy. It would cut through a few VIV rods. Then again, that was two hundred feet below, under a column of water. Which didn't make any sense.

But one thing she knew: she'd have to get past that second door to find the truth.

SEVEN

"THERE ARE NO MAPS OF FUSION LABS IN THE Island records."

Lucía was sharing her display with Joe, so he could see it for himself.

"Fusion was shut down a decade ago," he prompted. "Maybe they purged the records?"

"They've got drawings for every piece of tech, every building, even the power lilies and windmills floating a couple miles out, all the way back to the first plans for constructing the Island itself. No way they'd purge. There has to be a hidden file system."

"I can't help wondering *why*." Joe was just a voice in her ear as she sat in her garden-shack pseudo-underwater room, paging through the records. A cloud of brilliant blue tangs with their vivid yellow tails floated by on the wall display. "Why go to all this trouble to hide whatever's behind those doors? Why pretend the VIV never broke? They could just as easily have invented some innocuous explanation. Something that would have made you shrug and move along."

"You're a writer." She smirked even though he couldn't see her.

"And that's relevant how?"

"You're much better at thinking up ways to be sneaky."

"Ms. Ramirez, you really shouldn't flatter me so much."

She laughed lightly. They'd been at this half the evening, once she'd finished her work for the day, grabbed a quick dinner, and could get down to the business of sleuthing.

"Let's look at it from their point of view, then, shall we?" Joe's tone was serious. "That pesky new engineer Ramirez has stumbled upon our diabolical scheme. We could make up some story, but what if she doesn't buy it? She's wily, that one. What if she keeps looking into it? No, if we deny everything 100% from the start, either she'll think she's hallucinating and give up trying to figure out what's real and what's our carefully constructed lie or..." He just stopped.

"Or?" She prompted, a laugh still bubbling in her chest.

Joe's voice was softer. "Or... we'll say she's mentally unbalanced and have medical grounds for putting her on forced disability. Mandated therapy. A medical coverup."

A chill ran through her. Because that was one of the few ways you could remove a power engineer. Employment protections were very strong.

"Will you come visit me in the psych ward?" She couldn't disguise the weakness in her voice.

"Yes," he said quickly, then, "No! We're not letting that happen. I'll go full whistleblower at that point."

"I think you have to be an employee to be a whistleblower." But the smile was back on her face.

"Whatever." His voice was rough. "Okay, maybe no hacking into the secret records. Too dangerous."

"Agreed." She zoomed out to a visual representation of the Island's massive record structure. It looked like a tree with a thousand thin-fingered roots and even more branches and leaves above. "The Island is a rabbit's warren of physical things. Half is under water, air ballasts, water cisterns, plumbing—all the normal workings required for what's basically a sparsely populated city. Those are the bones and arteries that hold it up and keep it alive. But it's *also* a nervous system—power generation, wiring, cable running everywhere, the central processors, the battery banks for storage—"

"Ah-ha! They can try to hide a laboratory behind a locked door..."

"...but they can't hide its power usage."

Joe sighed. "Fools. They would have been smarter to make up a story."

"Yeah, well, let's see if I can actually find it." She was on manual controls, so she swiped away the graphical display and brought up the section with power usage logs. The data was massive and complex. She'd have to write some quick code even to query what she wanted—and she wasn't sure what she was looking for. Unexplained usage? That could be merged into the noise from other areas of the Island. Micro surges when it was turned on? That would be harder to mask. But if Johannes was actually doing crazy do-it-yourself fusion work, that would take substantial power, and there would be no hiding that load. Plus, it would throw off the careful balancing the grid AI had to perform to match storage to demand. Why Miller would endanger all that to cover for Casimir, she had no idea. They had to be connected, though.

"Lucía?"

"Hm?" Her brain was deep in the code.

"I think I found something."

She quickly pulled in two snips from some prior mods she'd written and sent the whole thing off to scour the Island's grid. Then she swiped open the image Joe had sent her. It was a picture of a dozen scientists gathered around a Tokamak style reactor. The caption read *Energy Island* (2035). "Where'd you find this?"

"In a *book*." He seemed inordinately proud of that. *"The Doomed Hunt for Free Power*. It's a historical dramatization, but check this out." The reactor image was replaced by a map. It was a complicated string of rooms that really did look like a rabbit's warren, pockets connected by tunnels, some leading to the surface.

Lucía zoomed it, trying to decipher it, but the resolution was low. "Can you tell what this is?"

"It's labeled as the reactor 'complex.' I think this part is the main room in the picture." A floating glow point hovered over one chamber. "But you know what this means, right?"

"What?"

"There's another entrance. Maybe several."

Lucía smiled. "Of course. The technology wasn't *secret* back then—hundreds of scientists were working on the project at the time." She searched through the Island's records for current maps, which included none of the fusion laboratories but had everything else. "I've got the coordinates for the spot above the damaged VIV. I should be able to match that to the chamber on your map, then overlay a current day map of the Island..." The auto-overlay pinned one map to the other, but then she had to manually scale and rotate it, taking her best guess at how far the rabbit warren of fusion research extended across the island. "And... there." She highlighted two spots where entrances to the warren lined up with current-day buildings. "A lot of the older buildings topside were torn down once the Island was transitioned to green tech only. Dormitories were replaced by desalination domes. Laboratories were swapped out for farm space or transformed into..." She was tapping up the geodata as she spoke. "The cafeteria. Looks like one of these connects to the basement of Chef's kitchen."

"Can you get in there?"

"Probably." She scanned a second entrance.

"This other one comes up under the admin building."

"Yeah, steer clear of that."

"All right, I'm on it." Lucía pinned the coordinates of the entrance to her locator, set up a homing pointer, and slipped on her boots.

"Wait, right now?"

Lucía glanced outside—it was getting dark. "Cover of darkness, right? Except I'll probably just walk right in and ask Chef if I can raid the pantry." She checked her pocket for the mini-light she always carried but then had another thought—she'd swing by her dockside workshop first.

"Just be careful."

She smiled. "I'll dial you in if I find something." She closed the chat channel and headed out. The ocean breeze was steady across the Island, no signs of gustiness, and clouds in the distance made the sunset spectacular. *Red sky at night, sailors' delight. Red sky at morning, sailors take warning.* Southern California had westerly winds, so the wisdom of the ancients applied here. High pressure, stable air mass to the West, so probably no storms tonight. Of course, the Island lived by up-to-the-minute weather forecasting fed by unfathomable amounts of data, sensors, and satellites all over the globe. No alerts had shown up on her display, and they always got plenty of warning. Still, it was a good visual check. Getting caught in a weather lockdown while *investigating* would not be good.

A quick swing by her workshop, and she picked up a dive light—more powerful than her mini lamp—and a tool she kind of loved but had little chance to use. The Flamejet Torch was just a burst of solid fuel and oxidizer, really a mini solid-fuel rocket if you got right down to it, but it produced a small, super-hot flame-blade. For any regular cutting, she would use an acetylene torch, but this was good for small, emergency-type cutting, worked underwater, and was the size of a stylus. Four bursts per canister—she tucked three into her pants pocket, along with some safety glasses and a pair of gloves in her back pocket. Not too suspicious. Maybe.

She strode off to the cafeteria.

It was past 8pm, long past dinner. With any luck, Chef Kyana would be cleared out.

Her luck wasn't that good.

Lucía peeked into the kitchen. It was stainless everywhere, some kitchen-purposed bots who did food prep, a massive amount of equipment, but mostly a half dozen cook stations with their articulated arms, performing a dance of precision stirring, mixing, and assembling on their individual stove/counter combos. A whole herd of hospitality bots was lined up at the back—one had delivered her dinner earlier.

Chef Kyana—Lucía didn't know her last name, that's all her nametag said—stood next to one of the cook stations, her sharp, dark eyes watching the bot's every move. It scooped up something it had just finished sautéing—smelled like onions—and dumped it into a bowl of dark and spicy-smelling liquid. Then it snatched up the bowl in its mechanical fingers and held it to the chef. She took a taste, her white plastic spoon brilliant against her dark skin, then she chastised the bot. "No. The caramelization is not complete. Set sauté time discriminator to one shade increment darker on visual and take a refract measurement for sugar content. To my specification." The bot dumped the onions into the disposal and grabbed another whole one to chop from a basket hanging nearby.

Chef Kyana swiped something into her display.

Lucía cleared her throat, but the chef jumped anyway.

She whipped her head around, dark curls bound up in a hairnet but swaying with the sudden motion. Then she straightened her crisp white jacket and frowned. "Did you not get your meal delivery?" She scowled at the hospitality bots like she was ready to send the guilty one to the reclamation center.

"No, that was fine. Loved the pasta, er, carbonara?"

Chef Kyana waved that off. "It was barely acceptable." She narrowed her eyes, inspecting Lucía. "Was it too rich for you? I downloaded your history, from Oregon. Mostly vegetarian. I'm concerned about the bacon."

"The bacon?" Lucía felt like this conversation was running away from her.

"In the carbonara!"

"Oh, um, it was fine. Really."

"It's synthetic, just like all the meat on the menu. Unless you have a health issue? There's nothing in your file."

"No, nothing like that."

"Then, you eat meat."

"Well, not much, but—"

"I can custom anything you like, but you must tell me. At least a day ahead."

"No. It's... the food is fabulous, Chef Kyana."

The intensity of her stance softened a little. "The food is rarely fabulous. But it is healthy and balanced and fresh. It should bring you comfort and energy. And, if you are very lucky, you will taste a little of the love I put into it."

Lucía smiled. "I can definitely tell."

"Then, why are you here?"

"Snack?"

"What?"

"I... just... wanted to maybe take a peek in the pantry and see if I could make a little snack. For myself. To eat."

Chef Kyana was looking at her as if she'd proposed slaughtering a pig in the middle of her pristine kitchen.

"Or I could just come back—"

"You wish to cook?"

This was turning into a disaster. "No, no! I just would, um, browse?" What was she thinking? She should have just broken in after Chef Kyana went home for the night. Wherever home was. For all Lucía knew, she slept in a cot in the cellar.

"I will increase your portions in the next meal." Chef Kyana was already swiping up modifications to Lucía's meal plan.

"I... um... okay." She should simply retreat as quickly as possible.

Chef Kyana waved her toward a door at the opposite end of the kitchen, still busy scanning something on her display. "You may 'browse' in the pantry. Further stores in the basement. There are walk-in refrigerators and freezers on both levels."

What? Lucía wavered. Was she just letting her pass? As Lucía edged forward, Chef Kyana's gaze whipped to her. "Do not eat the pudding. That is for tomorrow."

"No pudding. Got it. Thanks!" She hurried out of the kitchen, but Chef Kyana had already dismissed her and was berating the bot again.

Lucía quickly found the steps to the basement. From there, she followed the homing pointer on her locator. It took her into a chilled room that was floor-to-ceiling racks of produce in bins. It must have been something else in a prior life because it didn't seem like a refrigerator—the tiled floors and walls, with cooling coming from overhead units, seemed more like a repurposed lab. At the far end was another door, but this one was latched shut with a steel bar. There wasn't a control pad on the wall, but the door unlatched and swung open when she tried it. The short tunnel beyond it was dark. She pulled out her dive light. There were light fixtures overhead.

"Lights on," she tried, but they stayed off. Her motion didn't set them off either, but the tunnel was barely four steps between the chill-room door and another one, this time with a control pad. Her key manager stored keys for all the buildings on the Island, at least the ones she needed access to—no private quarters or offices, of course, but most major buildings and workshops. She stepped closer, and when it didn't click unlock, she tried to bring up the holographic keypad, but nothing would trigger it. Maybe it was powered down, like the lights. She tried the door handle, an old-fashioned paddle-kind, but it was locked. She stepped back, brought up the Island's grid on her display, and tracked down the power to this particular node. It took some searching, and then she had to authorize turning it on, but a second later, the overhead lights and the keypad lit up. She brought up her key manager and sent a command directly to the control pad, rotating through all the keys she had, not just the ones expected based on location. After a moment, the door clicked open with a key tagged as an older version of the fusion labs.

Okay, then. She pulled the door open.

The passageway beyond was dark. Her dive light showed a simple, paved concrete tunnel. After some steep steps down and a left-hand bend, the tunnel opened up into a room. Her light couldn't reach the end, but it was *huge...* and filled with batteries.

What? She opened her voice channel to Joe. "Are you there?"

"Been literally counting the seconds."

"Not *literally.*"

"Was starting to think you'd been caught." He actually sounded worried.

Which almost made her laugh. Then again, she was breaking into places that were probably locked for a reason. She slipped her headset cam out and clipped it to her ear, shining the light in tandem with the camera. "Can you see this?"

"Yeah. No idea what I'm looking at, though. Where are you?"

"In the rabbit warren." She strode closer to one of the large black boxes, half the size of her garden shack. "These are flow batteries. The big ones, like we have all over the Island. They're the main storage for load-shifting the energy the Island produces." As she got close, she could hear the faint clicks of relays in the banks and the hum of electrified wire somewhere. "And it's live."

"Live? But there's no power for lights?" Joe's voice floated over the weird scene, row after row of storage capacity with only her flashlight to show the scope.

"Really strange." Then she noticed the coolness

of the air—active temperature control, just like the normal battery banks, which kept them from overheating during the massive charge and discharge they went through every day. "But someone's maintaining this. I don't remember seeing anything like this on the Island's normal power capacity charts. Not my area, but still."

"Is this the room that was behind the locked museum door?"

"No." Lucía brought up the homing pointer on her display. "It's at the other end of the warren." She followed the pointer, passing the rows of batteries. Another door connected to a short tunnel and yet another massive room filled with the giant boxes. "Maybe this is all just excess storage," she said as she picked up the pace, jogging past the battery banks. "I mean, it makes sense to use up underground space we're not currently occupying."

"Maybe." But he seemed skeptical. "Seems like that wouldn't be hidden. Doesn't account for your broken VIV, though."

She reached another door at the end of the cavernous room, but it was locked. The pointer was getting close. "The other side of this door is only another fifty feet to the target." The keypad was powered, but none of her keys worked.

"Can you hack a keypad?" Joe asked.

"I thought you didn't want me hacking into things." But she was already getting out her torch.

"Seemed dangerous before we were in hidden underground caverns filled with mysterious batteries."

"We?" She smirked as she powered up the torch.

"Partners, remember? Okay, what are you doing?"

She'd pulled on her gloves and slid on her safety goggles. "There are three points of contact for most doors. Two hinges and the door lock. Usually made of metal. I have something that melts metal."

"That *melts…*"

She held her dive light with her teeth and fired up the torch.

"Holy shit!" It probably whited out her head cam. "Lucía, are you okay?" Joe was shouting.

She winced against the abuse on her ears but kept her focus on burning through the door lock. She couldn't talk with her dive light in her teeth, and she couldn't focus enough for CBT. Plus, she had to switch out another cartridge to get through the lock. But it only took a few more seconds, so she figured Joe could wait. Probably should have warned him, though.

By the time the second cartridge ran out, the door's lock was a dribble of metal down the front. She powered down the torch and took the dive light out of her mouth. "Sorry about that."

"What did you *do?*" Joe was still panicking, and it shouldn't make her laugh, but it did.

"I think I got us in." The door was metal and probably conducting, but not too hot for her gloves, and it looked like it would swing free. She had to grab an edge to pry it open, since the door handle was too hot and half-melted anyway. When she finally got it moving, she swung her dive light forward, expecting great things...

Just another short passage and a door beyond.

"Well, that's disappointing," Joe said.

She sighed. "I've got two more cartridges—" An alert popped up on her display, blaring red and demanding attention. It was a message from... "Oh, shit."

"Oh, shit, what?" Joe asked impatiently. "More *oh shit* than melting a door? Or some new *oh shit* I need to worry about?"

Miller was messaging her. She quickly opened and scanned it. "Oh, no."

"Oh, no, *what?*" Joe's voice pitched up.

"Miller knows I'm down here. He's telling me to

come topside. Right now." Her heart lurched, and she cast the beam of her dive light all around the room behind her and the short passage ahead. "There must be cameras. Or a silent alarm. *Shit.* How else could he know I'm down here?"

"Maybe he doesn't." But Joe didn't sound convinced. "Maybe he's just guessing. What does it say?"

"Bring the blow torch with you."

"Oh... shit."

"Gotta go." Lucía shut down the channel—no sense in dragging Joe into this *more*—and then she stared for a moment at the locked door in front of her. *So close.*

She turned and retraced her steps, walking faster and faster as she went.

EIGHT

ONE DAY SUSPENSION.

On the one hand, it wasn't much punishment at all. Lucía had to leave the Island, and it would go on her permanent record, but really... a slap on the wrist. On the other hand, her face burned with the shame of it. Or rage. She wasn't certain.

No, she was sure: *rage.*

The way Miller treated her like she'd betrayed the entire Island, and thus the mainland's critical source of power, and likely was a traitor to her country as well. She couldn't be trusted. She *disappointed* him. And then he frog-marched her down to the dock and put her on a Coastal Patrol boat, rushing her off the Island in the glooming night, as if she were a clear and present danger. *Even if* she was chasing a mystery that was nothing in reality. Even if she was poking around where, maybe, she didn't precisely have clearance. *She was a power engineer.* What the hell? If everything was so innocent and normal, why didn't he just explain what was going on in those closed-off sections of the Island?

Because it wasn't innocent. Or normal.

She knew that in her bones.

Which meant she wasn't just dragging her sorry ass and her backpack to Wicket and Jex's home—she was bringing whatever mess she'd stepped in.

Anxiety twisted her stomach while the rage-shame still burned her face. Whatever Joe might say —that she shouldn't worry about how the rest would react—the truth was she'd spent less than 48 hours actually at the cottage. Hardly any time at all. Getting tossed off the Island would take the shine off her "hero" status real quick. And it wasn't like she was bringing any answers about their power outages back with her. Joe was sweet, and kind, and damn adorable when she was honest, but he was obviously *flirting* with her all the time. He would say nice things. To her. About her. About his family under-standing her situation.

That didn't make them true.

She stepped off the autobus and hauled herself

up to Jex and Wicket's fairy-tale cottage. She was still wearing her Island work clothes. Miller had barely let her retrieve her backpack, no time to change into civilian clothes. When she reached the acrylic-shielded porch, she squinted against the blaring light by the door. She had the Ultra Black goggles Joe had given her, but she'd accidentally left the biohaz ones at the cottage, so she just squeezed her eyes shut and waited for the anti-viral dousing. Instead, the zip sound of the shield sliding away jolted her. She opened her eyes to find Joe spilling out of the doorway and Wicket holding the door.

"Are you okay?" Joe demanded, skidding to a sudden stop just before he nearly plowed her over.

She'd messaged him her ETA from the boat but kept it text-only. "I'm fine." She just shook her head, ignoring his worried face and awkward hands that tucked under his arms.

"For crying out loud, give her room, Joe!" Wicket beckoned her from the door.

Joe stepped back, even though he wasn't crowding her, and Lucía thudded heavy steps into the warm yellow light of the house. Wicket slipped her backpack from her shoulder and ushered her into the front room. Jex was there, chatting with Amaal, although they fell silent when she entered. A cup of tea sat on the small table next to the overstuffed armchair by the window—the one where Joe usually sat. The tea was steaming, but all Lucía could see was the cup's unbroken china, unlike the one she'd smashed during the power outage.

Everywhere she went, things... *broke*. How could it *not* be her?

Wicket insisted she sit in Joe's chair. Apparently, the tea was for her.

A swell of emotion blocked out the rage-shame in her face. "Thank you," she choked out. It embarrassed her to have such a reaction over *tea*. But the smell of it—sharp and black—yanked her back to all the times her mama would bring her a cup, when she was sick or upset, although Lucía couldn't imagine what had made her eight-year-old self distraught during those perfect Island days. Sometimes they would just sit, sipping and talking, her about the otters and their mischief, mama about her research and the drama in the lab.

Lucía sat, slowly, in the chair. The steam curled in misty tendrils into the air.

"I just finished making a cheese pastry," Jex offered.

"I..." She looked up, wanting to say something about the tea, but words were gummed up in her throat. "I don't think I can eat right now," she managed. "Thank you."

Amaal tilted her head, and Jex retreated with her to the kitchen.

"You just rest right there," Wicket said, a flurry of hands to keep her from moving. "I'll put your stuff in your room—" He was cut off by a rapid thudding of footsteps down the stairs.

Yoram careened into the room and stopped. "I'm not late!" He grinned, his slender frame light on his toes, black curls falling across his forehead. Then he took in the room, and his face fell. "Am I?"

"No cozy time tonight." Wicket waved him out with both hands, hustling him back up the stairs. Yoram's look of confusion dug into her chest. The cheese pastry wasn't for her, it was for Cozy Time with Wicket.

"I've ruined it, haven't I?" she asked Joe.

He had pulled a chair close then leaned way over, physically more near to her than the chair really allowed. "They're all worried about you."

"I feel bad about this." Ruining cozy time could be the least of it. They had no idea.

"Don't."

She pulled in a deep breath and let it out slow. She hadn't let herself breathe since that terse message from Miller. "It's just one day. I can go back." She was mostly muttering to herself. Could she fix this, whatever it was? Keep it from spreading to the family?

Joe nodded, waiting, his eyes measuring her the way they did the first time—like he was cataloging everything about her, maybe to put into that story he was writing. The one about a future world where there were no pandemics or wildfires or refugees, but he was struggling to work out how to make it realistic. Which seemed like the opposite of what he should do—why ruin the fantasy? But she didn't say that. "Everything okay here?" she asked, instead. All her drama and the "investigation" had taken up the oxygen in their relationship—whatever that was at the moment—and having a family wasn't just about having someone care for *you*. It was caring for *them*. She should have been asking more about everyone. Maybe that's why her connection to her family in Oregon had fallen apart—why the problems she brought home had them distancing when she needed them most. She was just *no good* at this.

"Well, Amaal's working too many hours at the Refugee Retraining Institute." Joe leaned back a little, his gaze less intense. "She just got another grant approved, but she's stressed because a whole new boatload from Baja showed up, and she's scrambling to get people fed. Meanwhile, Jex broke some new record on his channel with a cherry popover recipe, and now he's having an existential crisis about how much sugar he's encouraging his watchers to consume. Yoram's done with his semester design project and is starting his summer internship with some famous Island Designer. I think he's got a new girlfriend, but no one's seen her yet. And Wicket's picked up a few more hours of watching Eva while Maria's working extra hours at the hospital. There's some new sickness everyone's worried about there, so she's spending nights in decontamination before she comes home. Just to make sure the family's safe. And I finished that chapter I was working on! Threw an explosion at it, and that blew everything up nicely. But none of us are, you know, *actually* burning down doors and getting kicked off Power Islands for espionage—you're the most exciting thing around." He tried a small smile, but it seemed tentative.

She'd picked up her tea and cradled it, letting it warm her hands and taking sips as he filled her in. The tea was soothing the knot in her stomach, but only a little. She lowered the teacup to rest on the arm of the chair. "I shouldn't be dragging you into all this."

He leaned forward again. "Are you kidding? Please drag me into this."

She laughed a little, then shook her head. All the flirtation was fine, but this was serious. Far more serious than she thought. Serious enough that, maybe, she should be thinking about leaving. Before anything went further wrong. "Joe... what are we doing here?"

"Me? I'm hoping to date you, but I'm just now figuring out you're probably out of my league. You? I'm not entirely sure, but I'm worried."

He had blazed right past *dating,* but all right. They could deal with that later. "Worried about what?"

"I want you to be okay. You're one of the good things in this world, and it's not okay with me when the good things get hurt."

"I'm not hurt." But she was tired and beat down. Which meant she was in no shape to make big decisions right now. Decisions like leaving the cottage before she got everyone tangled in her mess.

"I've got a bad feeling about this," Joe said.

"Yeah. Me too." She set the tea back on the table. "I need some time to regroup. Think this through."

"Can I help?"

"In the morning."

"Fair enough." He stood and offered his hand. "Partners?"

He knew better than the rest how bad this might be, and yet he was still offering to help. It surged back some of that emotion from before. Comfort? Or just *care.* The way it was supposed to be.

And she couldn't say no to that. "Sure," she managed, and they shook hands, for real this time. His grip was warm and strong, reassuring, but not lingering. Not strange or even awkward. And it could have been, especially with the "dating" comment. Then he helped haul her out of the big cushioned chair her body had kind of melted into. She appreciated all of it. The simple openness of it. The honesty. And the fact that he was letting her go with a wave and a smile, not pressuring her in any way.

It was a small thing, but it was everything.

She dragged herself up the stairs, and after cleaning up and getting ready for bed early, she messaged Tito, just to check in. She was overdue. And he should know she was already hip-deep in trouble. *Again.* Because Plan B was always going back to Puerto Rico.

Lucía snuggled under the fluffy comforter of her bed and sent a message to him. *Hey, are you up?*

They were three hours ahead, so it had to be past midnight.

Hey, mija. Just turning in. How's the new job?

Can you do voice? she messaged back.

A second later, an incoming voice channel blinked at her. She tapped it open.

"Everything okay? You need me to come get you? *Mija,* I'm coming to get you. I'm booking a flight right now—"

"What? ¡Ay, Dios mío! *Stop.* Why you freaking out on me?"

"You're *calling* me, girl."

"That doesn't mean the world is on fire!"

"No? I watch the news. Your whole state is on fire! *California.* I told you that place was a damn mess. No good for you. What happened?"

"I got suspended. Just for a day. It's no big deal."

"*What?* You are the *nicest* person. And the smartest. What could you have possibly done? You know what, don't tell me. I'll just come out there and kick their ass. All of them. Then you come home. I'm coming to get you now."

"Tito, no!" *Home.* She wanted home to be *here.* That was the entire problem. "Do *not* come get me. Just stop it. I will hang up this call right now."

"I know you, Lucía. You play it all cool, like *no*

big deal, cuz, it's all handled, but inside, you're still hurting from this pendejo up north. And that family? What kind of familia doesn't look out for you, huh? You know who always looks out for you? *Me.* And Primo Eduardo. And your Tío Luis! You know how many times I had to stop him from driving to the airport to come murder that pendejo? Five. *Five,* Lucía. Not counting the time Benita threatened to hurt him, *bad,* if he came after you again. She said she'd cut off his—"

"Oh, my God, Tito!"

"I'm just saying. Your tía loves you. We all miss you, mija. Just come home."

Lucía sighed, audibly, so Tito wouldn't run off at the mouth again. She loved them all, but that *energy* just overwhelmed her sometimes. Tito said she had that same fire in her, that it was in her puertorriqueña blood, but she never quite felt it. Puerto Rico was the family that *had* to take her in. She wanted one where she got to choose—and who would choose her. Not people obliged to have her, even if their love was real. "I want it to work here, Tito, you know? I can't just give up. I don't want to let them run me off. Not again."

He sighed and was quiet a moment, which was huge. Lucía just hung in that space, the silence a balm to her soul. "It's your work," he said, finally. "It's important. I know that, I do. I just don't think..." He was holding back the words he wanted to say.

"That I can make it here." A little of that fire kindled up inside her.

"No, no, that's not it. You just need someone looking out for you."

"I'm a grown woman, Tito."

"Mija, don't hurt me like that."

That twisted the knife. And she knew he meant well. Wasn't that what she wanted? Wasn't that all she was after? A family who would *care* for her? Was it so bad to have that be Tito and Luis and Benita? She would have to give up her dream of working on the Power Islands—Puerto Rico was straight in hurricane alley, and no *floating* islands could withstand that—but she could find work as a power engineer in New San Juan. The population was dwindling every year as refugees came to the mainland, but the people who remained needed reliable power more than ever.

"I will always love you, Tito. All of you. But I *like* it here. I love my work. I don't want to give it all up because I'm just..." *A damn mess.* But she couldn't say that. He'd be on the first plane to LA. And that was part of it. She couldn't ever completely

be herself with him or the rest of her familia there—
they would work too hard to save her from it. Just
like they had all along. "I need to give it some time,
okay? See if it can work. This family is good. *Really*
good. I don't know, maybe they won't want me, but I
want to try. Okay?"

There was a stretch of silence. "If they hurt you,
I'm not going to be nice this time. I will come out
there, and if they are *very* unlucky, I will bring Luis."

She smiled. Because she would never let him do
it, but even if she didn't want him to save her, it felt
good to know he absolutely would. "Okay, I'm going
now."

"You message me. Let me know how it goes."

"I will." She closed the connection.

She hadn't even told him about Joe, which to be
honest, was for the best. And he didn't need to know
about the broken VIV and the underground batteries
and the mystery of what was happening in the old
fusion laboratories. There was nothing her overpro-
tective familia could do about any of that. Even
involving Joe was a risk—maybe she really should
walk away. This was so much worse than having a
stalker who just harassed *her*. If she kept pushing, all
of it might come apart in ways she couldn't even
imagine right now.

Her head had the kind of fuzziness that came when she'd worked a problem too long—what she said to Joe was the closest to the truth. She needed to rest and regroup.

She told the lights to dim, snuggled into her covers, then took one last glance at her messages. Her formal reprimand from Miller had come through. *Lucía's authorized access and damage to...* she didn't bother to read the rest. The others were form messages—turtle maintenance report, solar lily power gen for the day, the Chef's menu for the week, and... She blinked and roused from her half-asleep state. The query she'd sent off earlier to scour the power grid records for anomalies. It had come back, but she'd been too busy breaking Island protocols to notice. She tapped it open, but it was a deluge of information. She'd need a fresh brain to sort through it all.

But as she swiped it away, a strange sort of calm came over her. This was a solvable problem. It *had* to be. And she had a whole day to figure it out...

Tomorrow.

NINE

THE KNOCK AT HER BEDROOM DOOR WAS SOFT.

"Come in!" Lucía was deep in her analysis. The Ultra Black goggles gave her a whole new way to tackle the data. Joe had set up a virtual analysis chamber in her own virtual base with a dozen screens. She stood, bare feet planted, in the most spacious part of her bedroom, between the bed and the open window. She could feel the sun on her face and smell a hint of the distant ocean, but visually, she was in a command center, manipulating data on a bank of displays as tall as her room. She'd left the mute plugs out, which is why she could hear the door open and feet pad in, even if she couldn't see who it was.

"Hey, chica! You look busy. I should come back."
It was Maria.

"Just a sec." Lucía swiped away a virtual screen full of data and pulled up another to take its place. Wicket had helped her train up an AI program to help comb through the data. It was looking for pattern-matches that might mean something, broadly to her specs, but then coming up with its own hypotheses about anomalies. She had to sort through the data dumps, decide if they meant anything, tweak the program parameters, then send it off again to chew through more data. She took a quick look at the most recent result, discarded that quickly, widened the search time frame, and sent it off hunting again.

Then she lifted her goggles, parked them on her forehead, and squinted in the sudden brightness. "Sorry, just had to..." She trailed off as she saw Maria wasn't alone—she'd brought the baby. "Well, hello there!" she said to Eva with a smile.

Maria had a heap of clothes draped over one arm, and the baby parked on her hip with the other. "Say hi to Tía Lucía!"

Lucía flushed. She wasn't anyone's tía.

Baby Eva was checking her out but had a mouth full of baby hand, so she wasn't saying anything.

"I pulled these out for you," Maria went on, tossing the clothes on the bed, and taking a seat, settling Eva into her lap. She didn't seem to expect Eva to say anything. The baby was probably too little—Lucía had zero idea when babies started to speak.

"These clothes are for me?" Lucía took a seat next to Maria and leaned over to check the clothes out. There was a lot more glitter per square inch than she was used to.

"I'm still getting back into normal clothes," Maria said. "All my pre-pregnancy stuff is just sitting there, doing nothing. You should use them."

"Thanks. That's very sweet." Lucía smiled at Eva, who was staring at her with big brown eyes, but then the baby ducked her head into her mama's long brown hair.

"Hey, you don't have to be shy," Maria said to her, rubbing the baby's back. Then she lifted her chin at Lucía's goggles. "How's the investigation going?"

"Slow. But steady. Wicket's code is a lifesaver."

"Yeah, he's crazy smart." Eva burrowed deeper into her hair, so Maria turned her attention there. "Hey, you, come out and say ¡Hola!"

Eva steadfastly refused.

"Don't take it personally." Maria cocked her head. "Joe said you were out of sorts."

"He did?" What did that mean? "I'm fine."

Maria's expression was skeptical. "You're home on a one-day suspension, chica. And Joe says you take your work very seriously." She gestured at Lucía with her baby-free hand. "I can see it myself." Baby Eva extricated herself from her mama's hair to look at her again as if checking Lucía out for herself.

"I just don't want to make trouble for everyone here."

Maria waved that off. "Don't worry about us." But then Eva suddenly leaned out of her mother's lap, reaching for Lucía. "Hey, where you going?" But then it was obvious she wanted to come to Lucía. To her surprise and no small amount of terror, Maria handed her over. "Okay, go see Tía Lucía."

Lucía managed not to drop the baby, and Eva stopped squirming once she was safely in Lucía's lap. She reached up and put a little slobbery hand on Lucía's chin. She grinned as she wiped the slobber away, then used her t-shirt to dry off Eva's tiny fingers. Eva just watched with wide eyes.

"You're a pro, I see."

Lucía huffed a short laugh. "This is literally the first time I've held a baby."

Maria gestured with both hands. "You're a natural! Almost as good as Tío Wicket."

Lucía looked up from the baby. "So he's not—" She shut her mouth because that wasn't a thing you asked.

"Not what?" Maria frowned, then her eyebrows lifted. "Oh, you thought..." Then she was possessed with laughter, the kind that had her rocking back on the bed, knees tucked, shaking everything. It drew a wide-eyed stare from Eva. "Oh, my God!" Maria was still howling, but she managed, through great effort, to eventually rein it in and sit straight again. "Oh. My. God. I can't wait to tell Wicket."

"Please don't." Lucía cringed.

Maria snorted at that. "Oh, I definitely am." She shook her head, her humor settling. "No, Wicket is not Eva's papa, although he is definitely the best tío a baby girl could want, isn't that right?" The question was directed at Eva, who was still clinging to Lucía like her mother had suddenly become suspect. "He was over the moon when Eva was born. Well, all the way along, really."

"So, you were here, in the family, before Eva?" Lucía hoped that was a safe question. She was already messing this up.

Maria drew in a breath and blew it out. "Let's

see... it's been three years now with the family. I had just graduated with my nursing degree, starting training, super busy. Amaal came first, then Joe, then me. A year later, Yoram. Then, about 18 months ago, I met Alejandro." She smirked and fanned herself. "He was *so* hot. Like *illegally* hot. Dude was a high-speed chase in a stolen Maserati. Girls would just watch him go by with their mouths hanging open."

Lucía couldn't help her short laugh, even though the past tense on this had to be something bad. Alejandro was obviously no longer in the picture.

"And he was a doctor too! Doing his residency at the hospital. Which was a serious strike against him. Doctors can be such assholes."

Lucía's grin was hard to contain. "So, you definitely didn't date him."

"Are you kidding?" She gave Lucía a look like she was re-assessing her intelligence. "I was all over that boy." She sighed with exaggerated longing. "He was ruined for anyone else once he was with me. He proposed four times!"

Lucía's smile dimmed a little, dread creeping in. "You kept telling him no?"

Eva squirmed and reached for her mama. Lucía handed her off, and Maria collected her into her lap again.

"I told him, *Slow down, chico! We've only been together for six months!* But he kept saying, *"Now, baby. I'm calling the priest!"* She sobered and smoothed back the dark hair on Eva's little head. "I should have listened to your papa and married him when I had the chance." The baby reached up a little hand and played with Maria's lips. She kissed the tiny fingers several times, dramatically, until Eva smiled and pulled her hand back.

Lucía was holding her breath, waiting.

Maria sighed. "Alejandro died. Rota-49. I didn't even know I was pregnant until after the funeral. That's the one thing I wish—that I'd been able to tell him we'd made a baby. He would have liked that so much." There was a little shine in Maria's eyes, but nothing like the tears welling up in Lucía's.

"I'm so sorry." It always felt inadequate. There was never anything you could say that actually mattered. Nothing that compared to the raw fact of death itself. She knew that, but she was always left wanting to say or do something more. Instead, she blinked back her tears as best she could without being too obvious.

Maria nodded and adjusted Eva on her lap. "I couldn't have had Eva alone. My family had already moved north, getting away from these damn fires and the heat. But Wicket and Jex are my family now, and Wicket couldn't have been more excited about the baby." She smiled a little. "He always wanted babies, you know? They just couldn't bring themselves to do it. Not with how things are. Plus, Jex had a rough time in the Pandemic Corps. He was a cook, but he saw some things. Rough stuff. Dying kids. Then *he* got sick and took a medical discharge. He couldn't do a family, not with babies the way Wicket wanted. That's why Jex started bringing us in. We're Wicket's family. And now, Eva! I was worried about Jex, that it might be too hard on him, but he's been okay. Sometimes, things work out even when they don't." She reached her hand to Lucía's and squeezed it. "And now you're one of us."

"Well, not yet. I mean, I want to..."

"You just got here. I know." She patted Lucía's hand and hoisted the baby up as she rose from the bed. "Just take it from me. Don't wait. You never know how much time you have."

Lucía just nodded and didn't try to speak past the lump in her throat.

With a little coaxing, Maria got Eva to wave goodbye, then they cruised out of her room. She should get back to her data analysis, but first, she hung up Maria's borrowed clothes. They were slinky and sexy and glittery. Not at all her style. But she could see Maria in them, dancing in a club with her gorgeous almost-fiancé, now Eva's papa. *Now gone.*

She slid the closet door closed. Maybe Maria didn't want the memories in her room. The odds of Lucía wearing them were approximately zero, but she could safeguard them until Maria wanted them back.

Lucía slid the Ultra Black goggles down and quickly checked the status of her data searches. They were still chugging away. What would she do if she found the answers she was seeking? Bring trouble into the cottage? When there was already heartbreak living here? She'd lost her family, but she was no different than anyone else. The bucket of loss was endless and constantly being refilled. She knew why babies like Eva were few. She understood why Wicket and Jax gathered up their family from the humanity that already existed, literal refugees and figurative ones. Because there were already enough strays. The world didn't need new puppies. Eva would never know her father—at least Lucía had memories of hers. He taught her how to use a regulator. He was always the last to wake up on the weekend, waiting until she came and jumped on him in his bed. The easy tears that came from those gauzy memories were *not* conducive to goggles. She parked them on her forehead again, wiped her eyes, and almost missed the soft knock at the still-open door.

It was Joe. "You okay?" He was frozen in the doorway, concern on his face, holding a small plate and fork with something that smelled deliciously cheesy and baked.

"Is that for me?" She smiled and willed the tears away.

"Yes!" Joe stepped into the room, tentative at first, then crossing over to meet her. "Jex has conjured an amazing broccoli soufflé."

"Wow, that looks good."

"It *is* good." He beckoned her to sit on the edge of the bed with him before he handed it over. "He insisted I try it before bringing it up to you. New recipe."

"So, you're my food taster now?" She joined him in sitting.

"Only the best for our newest potential family member."

She forked a bite, closed her eyes, and *mmm-ed* her way through it.

When she opened her eyes, Joe was staring hard at her. "Please don't do that."

She grinned. "What? I'm enjoying my soufflé."

"Okay, I asked *nicely.*" He mock scowled at her.

She stuffed another bite in her mouth to keep from laughing. It felt good, all of it. *Don't wait.* It was solid advice. But she wasn't ready for this thing with Joe to be more than flirtation. That would be one more complication, and she needed to sort out this mess with the Island first. Besides, she might end up leaving, and she didn't want that to be harder than it had to be. For either of them.

He kept chastising her with his frown. "I came up here to give you moral support, but if this is how it's going to be, I'll let Jex order me around the kitchen some more."

She finished chewing and tried to tame her smile before saying, "Sorry."

"No, you're not."

"No, not really." She took another bite.

The smile was creeping back on his face. "How's the *Mystery of the Fusion Laboratory* going?"

She finished the bite and set the plate on the bed behind her, careful not to get crumbs on Wicket's perfect comforter. "Good. I keep thinking about those giant flow batteries, sitting there, humming away, *obviously* connected to something, but I can't find them on the grid."

Joe was nodding along. "I thought you said you

could hide a laboratory, but you can't hide the power it takes to run it."

"Exactly. But apparently, you can. Or I'm missing something big."

"Like what?"

"I don't know yet. But let's say for a moment that Casimir has some kind of fusion experiment going behind that locked door."

"Are we sure it's locked?"

That brought her brain to a screeching halt. "I guess not. Never got far enough to find out. Or past Casimir."

"I'm just wondering, in case you go back. Are you going to try again?" All the humor had left his face.

She frowned. "I hadn't gotten that far." *Should* she be chasing this down? She physically wiped that away, sweeping her hand through the air like it was something on her display. "Forget about that for now. First, we need some kind of operational theory about what's happening. Something we can get data on, to really prove it. So far, all I've got is a missing turtle and some extra batteries—no physical evidence of anything."

"So, our theory is that Casimir is a mad scientist taking over the old laboratories locked away on

Power Island One and is doing fusion because...?" He arched an eyebrow.

She shrugged. "Let's just say he is and figure out if we can prove it. Then we can try to figure out *why*."

"I think he's got a pyramid scheme where he's conning investors in his super-secret fake fusion technology, which is actually two gerbils running on a wheel and powering the lights on the display."

"That's... *crazy*." She scrunched up her nose.

He held out his hands. "No worse than believing in the monetary system."

"I'm sorry?"

"Everything's a story. It's just a matter of which ones we believe."

"I believe in things I can touch. And that make *sense*." They were getting derailed.

A little of that smile came back. "How do you touch *justice*? Or *trust*? There are plenty of things that are real that are also only stories in our heads. As for things that make sense... your broken VIV doesn't."

She pursed her lips. He had a point. "It does. I just haven't figured it out yet."

He inclined his head. "It doesn't fit in your story. The things you believe in right now. The things you think are possible. *Yet.* So, you've got to expand that range of possibilities. What does your data search show?"

She sighed and flicked a glance at her notifications. The AI programs still hadn't come back with any more proposed solutions. She focused on Joe's earnest expression again. He *was* trying to help—he just came from the perspective of a writer, not an engineer.

"First, you have to understand how the grid works," she said.

"I definitely don't." But he was waiting for her to explain.

"The grid is a massive balancing act between supply and demand at all times," she started. "Eighty percent of our energy comes from green tech, like the Islands—wind farms, solar, the VIV—but that's very intermittent. Ocean energy is nearly constant, but the rest has a lot of variation. That's why storage is key. The huge flow batteries—the real ones, not the hidden ones in the fusion labs—are essential. Demand is constantly changing too, plus we're still getting everything electrified and connecting all the grids to get the power where it needs to go. But supply has to match demand on a minute-by-minute, even second-by-second basis, to keep everything running. Even if we had enough green power overall —which we don't, we're still building out capacity—if we don't have it at the right *time* and in the right *place,* it doesn't help."

"So, the grid's a giant bucket with holes that you have to keep filling," Joe said, "and if you don't keep it full, the power goes out."

She smiled. "Except you're matching voltage and frequency, not water, but that's pretty good. It's a lot more complicated, of course. Things like the inertia of the whole system, where it's just as hard to slow it down as to speed it up, and it's all coupled together, only dynamically, and the problems in one part can ripple through and cause major problems somewhere else. But the point is that it's *complex.* And constantly changing. Too massive for humans to manage."

"Sure. That's what we have AI for, right?"

"Yes. And even that's broken down into manageable parts. Each Island has its own AI to control the load it feeds to the larger city grid on the mainland. That AI balances with the larger regional one. And so on. The USEC—US Energy Consortium—coordinates it all. Which is why even the outages are carefully planned. We want to keep overall usage down but still have everything in balance. That's why you should have alerts for your outages. It just doesn't make sense to throw off the balance with unplanned outages."

"Great. So, if the VIV breaks, then the AI should know about it. And correct for it. Somehow? And that will show up in your data? Maybe?" He seemed tentative about that.

"The problem is the AI is a dynamic learning system. It's *constantly* compensating for a million different things and learning how to do it better." She frowned. "Miller actually said something about that. That the AI glitches out sometimes and creates unintended effects. That's what he said the power outage here at the cottage would have been."

"Is that possible?"

"I don't think so. I mean, the entire purpose of the system—what the whole network is targeting—is keeping the power *on*. Except for planned outages, but those are tightly controlled. There are multiple redundancies in the system to prevent unplanned outages. I mean... it might glitch out once, but it would *learn* not to do that again." She shook her head. "I still haven't figured out how the outages at the cottage are connected to the broken VIV. Or how that's connected to the secret fusion lab, except that it's directly above it. Maybe it's all coincidence."

"Except you're here on a one-day suspension for the high crime of poking around."

She frowned. "Right. Something's going on."

"Casimir and his fusion pyramid scheme. With gerbils." Joe smirked.

She rolled her eyes. "But if it's all for show, why does he have a huge complex of operational batteries in the empty underground labs?"

His smirk faded. "Good point."

"And if it's not for show, even if he's starting with the old designs and equipment that were decommissioned ten years ago, even if he's barely managing to crank the thing up and make a plasma of some kind, that takes massive energy. Where's it coming from?"

"The batteries?" Joe asked, hopefully.

She shook her head. "Well, sure, but the power had to be generated somewhere first, before it can be stored. And he's not siphoning it from the Island energy sources, at least not that I can find. The batteries *have* to be connected to the grid—either the Island grid or the mainland—but I can't find any sign of it. Unless he's getting power from somewhere *off-grid*. Which... that's starting to get really weird."

"Doesn't fit your story."

"No." The notifications on her display flashed. The results of her latest analysis were in. "I think he has to be connected to some normal power source in some way. And if he is, then I ought to be able to find it. It's just a matter of asking the grid's AI the right questions about what it's balancing and why." She swiped open the notification then sent a display mirror to Joe. He opened it up, and they sat side by side on the bed, looking at the same data on their own individual displays.

"I have no idea what this is," he said.

"Spectrum analysis of frequency deviation."

"I still don't know what this is."

She smiled. "I'm looking for faults in the micro-grids all around the Island. Basically, anything anomalous. But there's really nothing. Almost like... and I don't know how this is possible..."

Joe swiped away the display and turned to her, expectant.

She did the same. "Like someone's tampered with the AI."

"And that's unlikely?"

"Very. I mean, it's self-correcting, right? But then..." She frowned. "It should be detecting and correcting the outages here at the cottage. Even if it was a glitch, the social feedback alone should be enough to prompt adaptation within the AI."

Joe nodded. "Jex popped off majorly online a

couple weeks ago when it interrupted one of his shows. He was listing really high for a while. People were *pissed*."

She nodded. "No way it could miss that. And you guys filed complaints too, right?"

"For months. Not that it ever did any good. Obviously. And we're not the only neighborhood hit."

Months? A creeping feeling raised the hairs on the back of her arms. "It's on purpose." She turned away from Joe and brought up the grid network for the Island. "It's on purpose, they've tampered with the AI, redirecting its baseline target to..." She blinked. "It's not the outage—it's your *batteries*. They're draining power from the mainland batteries to pipe into the secret Island ones." She swiped the grid away and turned to Joe.

His eyebrows were hiked up. "Someone's hacked the power grid."

"I have no idea *how*..." But now she knew where to look. "But if they are, if this is how they're connected, then there has to be some way to get that power from the mainland to the Island. Not the normal lines. There's a dozen or more of them, subsea cables connecting the Island to the mainland, but they're all on the Island grid, and anything on the grid, I would see in the data. Unless that's masked somehow." She logged out of the Island system altogether and accessed the regional grid. She didn't have permission for everything, but she could bring up a standard map of the power lines hooking up the mainland to all the Islands up and down the coast. And when she matched up the ones leading out to Power Island One... "Holy shit." She mirrored it over to Joe.

"What? What am I looking at?"

"There are fourteen power cables that run from Power Island One to the mainland." She pulled in a breath and let it out slow. "Except, on the mainland's version of the grid map... I count fifteen."

"There's an extra cable."

She swiped it away and turned to him. "We just found our power source."

TEN

It took three tries for Lucía to tie up her boat to the solar lily.

The sea swells had some serious energy today. Her first day back on the Island and the forecasts were predicting a mild-to-moderate storm sweeping through by midafternoon. She needed to get these maintenance checks cleared out before that happened—and then she could go after the evidence she needed from the secret fusion labs.

The more she thought about that, the angrier she got.

People *relied* on power. Not just to connect to vital services, but to work, to learn, to keep their medical equipment running. Part of the whole tacit agreement to endure the rolling blackouts—which were critical to battling the climate crisis fueling the pandemics, which lay at the root of just about everything awful in the world, *including what killed her family*—was that it was *necessary*. Everything was in service of getting to net-zero carbon emissions. And the world really needed to go *negative*. Actively sequestering carbon out of the atmosphere was the only way to cool the planet and have any chance of reversing the damage already done. The US was *still* at 20% fossil fuel usage—definitely a laggard in the world; China reached net zero five years ago—but it was a little less every year. The USEC continued to build out renewable capacity, kept electrifying every possible energy use, and carefully balanced the grid so that no energy ever went to waste. But it wasn't moving fast enough. And it was a race against time. Even if the entire world got to net zero in ten or fifteen years, it might be too late. The melting of the permafrost, the destruction of species and ecosystems, plus all the human lives lost—so much of it was irreversible. Like getting oxygen to a patient who can't breathe... if you're too late, it doesn't matter.

Every power engineer knew this. Every person on the street understood. This was a world-wide effort, and everyone had to do their part. Scientists were hard at work, constantly researching new ways to battle both the plagues and the warming of the planet that drove them. Every kind of carbon sequestration tech was being researched, developed, and implemented. The Power Islands were just one piece of a fantastic globe-spanning effort to get to net zero. And then negative. Because that was the only way to put this genie they'd unleashed back in the bottle.

And implicit in that effort was the promise that the outages were necessary and the harm would be minimized—that meant backups and redundancies. The whole system was built on a mountain of trust that everyone was working together, sacrificing together, to make the entire operation work as best it could.

The idea that old man Casimir was running his own, personal rolling blackouts so he could play scientist in some abandoned labs on her Power Island... she'd been seething ever since that realization had settled on her like a shroud. He wasn't just stealing energy—he was corrupting the trust that everything relied upon. He was negating everything she and her parents had devoted their lives to.

Lucía carefully balanced her weight on the boat, taking in the rocking motion of the swells and reaching her gaffe hook toward the clump of kelp that had somehow gotten tossed up onto the fifty-foot diameter solar lily. Probably otters. They took refuge from the sharks in the kelp forest and liked to wrap themselves up to stay anchored. She could just see them screwing around, getting tangled, then dragging the whole mess up onto a lily pad.

The problem was getting it off again. It was hard enough to hook a kelp strand, but once she did, it just slithered out of her grasp. She gritted her teeth, wanting to stab straight into the mess, but that would damage the membrane, which was built to float and bend and flex with the waves, not take a puncture through the middle. Her frustration kept mounting until she was ready to climb out of the boat and go hands-and-knees across the membrane. Which would probably fold up around her and drag her down into the ocean with it.

Some things had to be done slowly, with precisely balanced patience, no matter how long that took, because that's just how physics worked, and it didn't give a damn about your righteous anger. She took a deep breath, hauled the hook back into the boat, and folded up her legs to sit on the floor. The small skiff was easily maneuverable, with a solar-powered motor that was light and just right for the job, but it wasn't built for comfort. She closed her eyes and let herself rock with the boat, absorbing the motion rather than fighting it. Gulls cried in the distance, a long chattering of calls that was some kind of squabble. The swells lapped at the side of the boat. A breeze brushed her face, whipping her hair around, telling her to be calm. The frustration settled, but her outrage was annealing into something harder, more determined.

Who knew how long Casimir had been siphoning energy? The good part was that she'd figured it out. Maybe Miller was covering for him— she still couldn't figure out *why*—but it was the kind of thing no one with any sense would stand for. She just had to get the evidence and then escalate it to the proper level, and it would be stopped. Then maybe things would settle down for her. She'd have space for Joe and wherever that relationship might be going. She could really get to know Jex and Wicket and the rest of them. They might even, in the end, if she didn't bring too much trouble into the family, decide to go forward with adopting her in.

Maybe things would be *good* for once.

She breathed in the briny air, let it out slowly, then opened her eyes and worked her way up to standing again, bracing against the side of the skiff. She squinted against the bright sheen of sun, reflecting in spots off the lily's glassy solar surface, and examined the tangle of kelp, a mass of floats, leaf-like blades, and slithery stipes. The long stems were like a pile of slick rope—she wouldn't get anywhere with that. Instead, she rocked with the waves, timing her hook so it slid past the tangle and rested under a particularly large, flat blade. Waiting for just the right moment, she flicked it up, *fast*, away from the surface of the lily, driving the hook through the blade. Then slowly, gently, she reeled the whole tumbling mess into her boat.

Once that was done, the rest of the maintenance check was trouble-free. She puttered the boat along, the motor sounds lost to the slapping of waves. Clouds were gathering a little earlier than expected, but they were still out at the horizon, plenty of time to get in and get busy with her evidence gathering.

Back at the dock, she sent a quick message to Joe, opening a voice channel.

"Well, if it isn't my favorite power engineer." His voice in her ear fired up her already determined stride.

"Yoram's going to be sad to hear that."

"Naw, the kid probably has a crush on you, too."

"Kid? He's like three years younger than you."

"An *eternity* in wisdom and experience, I assure you." He cleared his throat dramatically. "Unless you're looking for the more young-at-heart, then I can guarantee that my child-like wonder remains intact."

She couldn't help a muffled laugh. "I like a man who knows who he is."

"I'm definitely that, too." Then his tone got more serious. "Where are you? How worried do I need to be, on a scale of *Relaxing in My Room, Definitely Not Hacking the AI* to *Breaking into Miller's Office with a Blow Torch?*"

"Much closer to Number Two." She was making good time across the Island. "It's Friday. Casimir said he does tours for students then. There aren't any on the schedule, but I'm going to use that as my excuse to show up. He did actually invite me, after all. Can't decide if I'm going to try to talk my way into the back or just threaten him with the torch." The Flamejet was back at her dockside workshop, so that wasn't really an option. Plus, she wasn't into threatening people.

"A charm offensive could be very effective. Sneaky, too. I like it."

"I can leave the channel open if you'd like." She was getting close to Dr. Ellis's big glass-box building. "That way, you can supply witty zingers if I get stuck."

"Or I can call the Coastal Patrol."

That made her smile, and a warmth spread across her chest. She reached the door and paused with her hand on the bar to open it. "Okay, I'm here. But you should know something before I go in."

"What's that?"

"You're not out of my league."

"What? You tell me this *now,* right as you're headed into the den of vipers and mad fusion scientists? That is some *terrible* foreshadowing. Don't do that."

She laughed. "I take it back."

"Well, I wouldn't go that far."

She shook her head, grinning like a crazy woman. Or maybe just a happy one. "I'm going in," she said and pulled open the door. The interior was the same as when she was here before to see Astra Olson: the greenhouse plants with their attendant bots, the wide marble staircase, and the elevator with the *Museum of Fusion Technology* sign hanging above it. She strode up to the elevator and waved at the call button.

The sound of footsteps echoed around the entrance atrium, coming from the stairs. Lucía stepped back from the elevator and peered in that direction—maybe Casimir was upstairs visiting

Astra? But when the person belonging to the footsteps reached the landing of the stairs and turned to hurry down the second half of the flight, it was Astra herself, not Casimir.

Astra saw her and froze on the steps.

Lucía barely got out, "Um, I'm here to see—" before Astra was running away. Literally turning around and hustling up the stairs at twice the rate she came down. The elevator dinged its arrival as the sound of Astra's footsteps faded. Lucía stepped inside and pushed the button. Once the doors closed, she said, "That was really strange."

"Who was that?" Joe asked, keeping his voice quiet so it wouldn't be so obvious she was on chat.

"Astra Olson. Power engineer for the VIV. Couldn't run away from me fast enough."

"Weird."

She let that go without a response because the elevator had arrived, and the doors were opening.

Her mouth fell open, as well.

Giant black soot marks blasted out around the edges of the double set of doors. The James B. Ellis Fusion Museum sign above the door was covered in soot. The podium next to the door had been reduced to a pile of ash.

"Oh, no," she breathed. The scent of burnt wood and plastic assaulted her nose.

"*What?*" Joe sounded panicky. And she wanted to tell him, but she had to make sure she was alone. She tried the door, and it opened, but her hand came back grimy. Inside was an utter disaster. Everything was gone, blackened, or melted into a puddle. But there was definitely no one down here besides herself.

"There was a fire." Her voice was hushed as she stepped through the piles of ash. "Everything's gone." The hallway light barely reached into the room. She slid her base station from her pocket and turned on the light.

"*Holy shit.* They burnt it down? To keep you from finding out what it was?" The horror in his voice was creeping up her spine.

"We don't know that." But she couldn't escape the same conclusion. The coincidence was just too great. She passed a giant blob of metal on the floor, obviously melted down and then solidified as it cooled. *The old fusion reactor model.* "Would the curator of a museum really burn the whole thing down, just to stop me from finding his secret experiments?" She kept going, toward the door at the back, the place she'd been so determined to reach, and now dreaded to see what was beyond. "What if it was an accident? What if he was trapped in here when it happened? And why wasn't there anything on the Island alert system?"

"One-day suspension?" Joe's voice in her ear was archly suspicious. "Just enough time to clear out all the evidence."

"I mean, they could have just moved whatever they had going on." She was frozen, hand on the doorknob, now sooty and cold. "They didn't have to destroy everything."

"Maybe they did."

She pushed open the door and swung her light to shine into the room beyond. It was the same size as the one she'd just passed through. "There's nothing left. Everything's ash. Like the walls are literally peeling off."

"How did they keep it from burning down the whole Island?"

"That's a good question." She crept forward, stepping over a bunch of glass that had shattered and then melted in the heat, forming a crazy quilt of glittering spots in the blackness. Another door at the far side of the room led to a small hallway likewise covered in soot. "The fire was hot enough to melt the reactor in the museum. Hot enough to melt glass.

But somehow it was contained to these rooms?" At the end of the hallway was another door—this one stood partly open. When she pulled it, she recognized the chamber beyond. "I've reached the battery room. It's empty."

"Burning batteries sounds bad."

"I don't think the batteries were here." She strode into the larger room—it was sooty and blackened everywhere, but there wasn't much left on the floor, no debris. And more important, she wasn't passing out from toxic fumes. "Battery fires are incredibly dangerous. Explosive, toxic gas. I'm not choking to death right now, so I'd say no, the batteries had to be moved out before the fire."

"So definitely not an accident." Joe paused a second, then said, "Lucía, you need to get out of there."

"Yeah." She was already picking up her pace but not heading back to the museum. "I'm going out through the kitchen."

"Good thinking."

Fortunately, all the rest of the doors were unlocked—or, more accurately, they were burnt half away. The fire raged through all the way to the room just before the kitchen's storeroom. That door was intact but unlocked. It was the middle of the day, near lunchtime. She heard Chef Kyana cursing out instructions to a bot upstairs.

"Okay, I made it out of the rooms." Her hands and boots were filthy, and ash clung to her coveralls. She paused and looked back through the open doorway. "These rooms were initially laboratories for fusion reactor research. I bet they're wrapped in all kinds of fire containment systems, precisely to keep them from burning down the Island in case of an accident."

"That's great, but you really need to be nowhere near them right now."

"I don't have *anything*, Joe. No evidence, no nothing."

"I know, but they burnt down the place to stop you—"

"*Exactly!* What do you think I'm going to do? Just let that happen? Just let them get away with this? These... *cabrones*... they are stealing power. They are destroying the public trust in us, the Islands, the power engineers, the whole system. How are we supposed to keep the world from falling apart if they tear up the one thing that makes it work? And now they're destroying evidence of whatever this is, this ridiculous, selfish thing they are doing." She was pacing the refrigerated room, between the racks of produce. Her hand was clenched so hard around her base station, it hurt. She stopped, turned off the base station light, and stuffed it in her pocket.

"Lucía—"

"I'm going up through the kitchen. I'll let you know when I can talk." Then she cut off the channel because she needed to scream her frustration, and she couldn't do that with Joe listening. Or Chef Kyana, either. She marched back into the ash-filled cavern, closed the heavy door, and scream-growled in the dark for a minute. As she breathed in the soot-laden air, great giant gulps-full, willing her pounding heart to settle, the idea of what she needed to do slowly came to her. It crystallized into a plan she could actually implement. And it attacked the problem by reducing the unknowns—that was what she did best. *Solve problems. Take action.* Focus on that, and she would be okay. She could do this.

She opened the door again, marched through, and headed straight up to the kitchen.

Chef Kyana did a double-take. Lucía had to look like she'd walked out of the fire itself, still breathing flames, a dragon's energy moving her quickly through the kitchen before Chef Kyana could figure out something to say.

Outside, Lucía's stride was even more long and

purposeful. She waited until she was well clear of the cafeteria before opening the channel to Joe again.

"*Jesus,* Lucía, what's going on? What are you doing?"

"I'm going for a dive."

"What?" He wasn't outraged, just… confused.

A brisk wind buffeted her face, blowing away the ash still clinging to her. It felt like a blessing until she looked up—clouds were gathering overhead. The distant storm on the horizon had quickly blown in. She picked up her pace, jogging across the Island to get to the docks. Her dive equipment was there, but she would also need something else. *A camera.* The old-fashioned kind. She'd had her tools shipped down from Oregon, but she'd never had a chance to unpack everything. It should still be there.

"Lucía, I don't understand—"

"The only evidence left is down below," she said. "The VIV that they fixed? Somewhere in the VIV field is a shiny-new repair spot, the parts they stole to replace the broken ones under the lab. And there's that fifteenth power cable, the one that's not supposed to be there. They can erase the mainland's map, they can burn down a lab, but they can't rip up a subsea cable in 24 hours. And they probably didn't think they'd have to."

"You're still trying to get evidence."

She couldn't tell if he approved or not. "Yes. And then I'm coming home. I need to sort this out. I'll take what I can get here and then get out."

"Okay, I like the *getting out* part of this plan."

"This is bigger than I can handle alone." She bit her lip because it felt dangerous to admit that. Far more dangerous than going out for a dive in an oncoming storm to collect evidence of crimes committed by God-knew-who. "I'll need your help to sort this out. When I get back."

"You got it." He sounded nervous. "Lucía, be careful."

"I'm always careful." She'd reached the dock, so she slowed a little. She needed to catch her breath before going out. "I'll message you when I'm topside again." Then she closed the channel because she didn't want to hear anything that might talk her out of this.

She quickly dug into the massive pile of storage crates inside the dock's workshop—some hers, some belonging to the previous power engineer. She had to look through nearly every one before she found it. An old underwater digital camera. Not chip-enabled. Images stored on an obsolete format data card. But whoever was orchestrating all this—

Casimir, Miller, even Astra was probably in on it—couldn't hack something that was air-gapped from the rest of the grid. Just like they'd kept their whole operation separate, she'd get her evidence the old-fashioned way—physically going there herself.

And then she'd get out while she still could.

ELEVEN

THE IMPENDING STORM ABOVE WASHED THE color from the water below.

The kelp and the turtle tower were shadowed and murky. The schools of shimmery blue rockfish had lost their brilliance with the dimming of the sun. And the shadow the Island cast over the vast field of the VIV was even darker than normal.

Lucía swam to the edge of the constantly churning machinery, with its rods extracting the energy of the ocean to feed a hungry world. It was immense, and she was one diver on a seriously tight timeline. How could she possibly find the one spot where they'd made the swap, new parts for old? Her breathing was too fast—more than just the exertion of the swim—and she consciously tried to slow it as she hovered. The air-gapped camera was attached to her belt with a strap. She unhooked it, cinched the strap around her wrist, and practiced taking a few shots of the VIV. The camera was a little bulky with the spotlight attached, but it was neutrally buoyant. She had strapped a heavy-duty dive light to her headlamp, and that gave a nice, strong spotlight to wherever she was looking, but the camera needed a wider patch of illumination to give context to the picture. It wasn't designed for night-shooting, so having all three lights should help. She had to line up her headlamp/dive light with the camera's beam just right to get the autofocus to trigger at such low light. It took a few tries, but she got the hang of it. The camera was time-stamping everything, so that was good.

She kicked up to the top of the VIV and set out across it. Her first objective was to document the power cables. She could only assume the extra one—Casimir's secret cable—was located near the others. The map she'd seen was just a representation and probably meant to hide the reality—it wasn't like the 15th cable was labeled TOP SECRET CABLE HERE. You would never have known if you hadn't compared the maps. The actual geographical location of the secret cable could be anywhere. But she knew the official ones were on the dockside of the Island, closest to the mainland to minimize distance. They sat near the northwestern edge, bundled with the rest of the subsea power grid system. "Cables" weren't simply power lines—the subsea grid was comprised of transformers, switchgears, and a whole monitoring apparatus. If she were to lay down a secret cable for her secret experiments, she'd tap into those systems. She had no idea, really, how they could have laid a subsea cable at all without detection—that was a major undertaking, spooling a continuous cable long enough to reach the shore, anchoring it properly, much less attaching it at both ends to the rest of the grid. Plus, all the equipment, bots, and personnel needed? The mere fact of its existence was evidence of an operation much bigger than a lowly museum curator could pull off. Which was why she needed more than an extra line on a power map to say this actually existed. Especially now that the rest of whatever equipment they had on the Island had been removed and all evidence literally burned to ash.

The coolness of the shadowy water seeped into her, making her shiver just before her suit's heater kicked in. She scanned the VIV below as she swam, just in case she lucked into finding the spot where they stole the replacement parts. That still didn't make sense—how was the broken VIV related to the secret labs? It *had* to be connected because they'd tried so hard to erase it.

The constant thrumming of the VIV dimmed as she approached the cable station. A clearing on the ocean floor made room for the whole system. The Island technically floated, but it was anchored at several points to the continental shelf. The water tower at the center was key, structurally holding everything together and tethered at multiple points to pylons sunk into the seafloor. Tethers gave the Island some flex during storms like the one about to hit. The only other true anchor point was here, at the cable transfer box. A massive bundle dropped from the Island above, an umbilical of power falling to the ocean floor. Each of the individual cables was about a foot in diameter, but the bundle twisted together was a good five feet across, a giant rope that carried all the energy the Island produced. There was slack built into it, so it could take the movement of the Island, but it was anchored to the ocean floor, where it was unbundled, and each cable snaked away from the Island off to power the mainland.

Lucía lined up her lights and shot picture after picture, from every angle, swimming around the full circumference of the station. It wasn't until she got to the far side that she realized... an extra cable was literally strung up the side of the bundle that climbed all the way to the Island. Her heart pumped a little faster as she took extra pictures of that, trying to document every inch in case she missed some clue as to who did this. Real, indisputable evidence. And if they came and ripped the cable out later, she would still have the pictures.

She stopped, hovering near all those megawatts of energy pulsing through the lines, and examined the shots. In one, a bright spot shone from somewhere past the transformer boxes, inside the VIV. She looked at the orientation and swam back to where she'd taken it, lining up the shot. Something shiny in the VIV had caught the beam of her dive light. She tracked where it was, swam around again... and there, a dozen feet into the VIV field. *Brand new parts.* A whole section had been replaced, and the usual algae and barnacles and sea life hadn't yet been able to cover the brilliant sheen of the metal. She got as close as she dared, snapping a dozen more pictures, adrenaline surging through her even more.

This was it. This was the key that would unlock it all.

She was so excited, she was panting.

She pulled up from the VIV and tried to calm herself, reflexively checking her oxygen levels. 100%. Plenty of—*wait, what the fuck?*

Her heart rate zoomed. She didn't even have to do the math. She'd been down for—*how long, dammit?*—but that just kicked up her pulse even more.

Slow down. Think. She was gasping. Her oxygen was low. She'd been down for a while, but not long enough to use a full tank. Her indicators were obviously broken—her tank had to have been low when she started. She reached back to twist the valve for her emergency tank. *Nothing.* How could that—

She could barely suck in a breath... *fuck.*

She started swimming, angling up for an emergency ascent, strapping the camera to her wrist as she kicked.

How far?

She looked up, her labored breath loud in her ears. She was under the Island. Not in the center, but a quarter of the way in. She was already above the VIV, so the underside was only a hundred feet up, but that wouldn't help because there was no damn air under the Island. She had to get out of the shadow. And not panic. Rising reduced some of the pressure on her lungs, but she was still barely pulling in air. Her muscles were already screaming... *fuck, which way was the dock?* That had to be the closest air, and it couldn't be that far. She fumbled at her headlamp and dive light until they switched off. *Keep swimming. Don't stop swimming.* The camera's light bounced all around the dark like a crazed angler fish after its prey. She managed to shut that off too. Then, up ahead, she could see it—*a haze of light.* Outside of the shadow. She could see the outline of the tower of turtles. She just had to keep heading that direction. And rising. But there was less and less air...

Then nothing came in. Zero gas. Her lungs screamed, but all the air was gone. Her muscles were cramping. *Keep your respirator in.* She stopped swimming, closed her eyes, and focused. She needed help. Who could help? No one was here. Just her and the VIV and...

Turtles. She opened her eyes and used her CBT to open her files. Emergency mod. Somewhere. The world started to dim. Hypoxia. She couldn't find it. Her brain was confused. She had to *focus* and find the file. *There.* Sent. Then she clawed at the water, trying to move forward, but nothing worked. Everything was cramped and going numb. Her lungs were frozen, imploded, and there was no air. None. Dark was creeping in, tunneling her vision down...

She drifted. Back down toward the VIV...

Oh, God, she wasn't going to make it. Like Turtle 55, she'd wandered into the VIV, and she wasn't coming back out. Poor Turtle 55. No one would ever find his body. Just like hers, drifting into the deep, dragged out to somewhere. Then a thousand swirling things, all moving and tumbling, pinching her, grabbing her. She was going to die in the VIV. It would chew her up, and she'd wash *away... away... away...*

The world got brighter. Lighter. The heaviness of it all lifting. This wasn't so bad. Like falling up into a dream. Joe would want to know this. She should tell him. But it was too late for that—

The world broke in half. Blinding and rough, tossing and bashing, and *she was in air.* She flailed and tore the respirator out of her mouth. Great gulping gasps filled her lungs. She was blind in her mask. Water splashed all around her, in her mouth. She choked, still trying to get air. *Stay above the water.* She grabbed onto something cold and metallic. *Turtle,* her blurry mind told her. They were all around her, dozens bobbing in the water, flailing as much as she was, at the surface, where they didn't belong. They'd dragged her topside. *But not safe.*

Not yet. The waves were tossing her and the turtles, banging and splashing, threatened to drag her back under. Her hands were barely functional, but she shoved off her mask so she could see.

The dock was so close. The waves heaved her up and then down, violent in the storm. She kept her grip on the one turtle and fought the others. Their pinchers were still grasping hold of her suit, trying in all their turtle earnestness to beat the waves and drag her to the small side ramp next to the dock. Only twenty feet. *So close.* Another wave took her in the face, and she nearly swallowed ocean. Choking it out, she finally got her legs free enough to kick.

A woman stood on the dock.

"Help!" Another wave bashed her into the flotilla of turtles.

The woman didn't move. Didn't reply.

The turtles were holding her back now. Lucía grabbed harder onto the closest one and thought-commanded the emergency mod open again. She shut it down. They released her, all at once, leaving her flailing in the open water as they paddled their way back to the depths. She kicked toward the ramp. The woman was still there. Lucía just kept kicking and spitting out seawater—she had air, but she was hardly moving. The sea kept pulling her back.

Finally, the ramp was under her, but her equipment felt like it weighed a hundred pounds, holding her to the sea. She stumbled, lost her footing on the slickness of the ramp, falling back into the water. Then a hand grabbed her arm, hauling her forward. They were still in the water, but those hands unbuckled her gear, pulling it from her body and tossing it aside, back to the depths. It was enough to free her. The woman splashed ahead, dragging them both up the ramp. Lucía got her feet under her and finally staggered out of the water.

Only then did she see who it was.

"Why?" Lucía gasped, still struggling to get oxygen back in her body.

Astra didn't answer. She just grabbed Lucía's floppy arm and looped it around her neck, pulling her toward the dock. Lucía had to focus on making her legs work, so she didn't take them both down. One of her fins had been lost along the way, but the other was making every step awkward and precarious. She stopped briefly to tug it off, her feet cold in the windstorm still whipping around them. Astra brought her up on the dock, and Lucía thought she might let go, but instead, she turned them both right around and boarded a mid-sized bay boat, one used to do maintenance checks on the wind farm. Astra dumped her at the aft seating and went forward to the center console, firing up the engine and tapping something into navigation. Then she hurried past Lucía, back onto the dock, and got busy throwing off the tie-downs.

Lucía just watched, her chest still heaving, the weakness in her body and the cold of the wind making her shake.

Astra used a boat hook to push the boat free. Then she stood back and glared. "Just *go*," she hissed, her eyes wild and livid. "And don't come back!"

The boat lurched, the motor ramping up. The autopilot was guiding the boat out of the slip. Lucía suddenly remembered her camera, miraculously still strapped to her wrist. She held it up and snapped several pictures of an increasingly horrified Astra. She ran down the dock, chasing after Lucía and her bay boat, but it was too late—she was pulling away from the Island.

Astra stood at the end of the pier, hands clenched at her sides, obviously furious even as she receded too far for Lucía to see her expression. Then she turned and stomped away.

A lurch of fear—belated but still alive—clenched Lucía's chest. It was foolish to show Astra the camera. She might still come after her. Lucía stumbled forward and checked the destination and route Astra had laid in. *The mainland harbor.* The weather was still stormy, the boat rocking more as she pulled away from the Island, but it was passable. She slumped into the pilot's seat and briefly thought of calling the Coastal Patrol. Instead, she strapped in and modified the autopilot to max speed.

She sent a message to Joe to meet her at the Huntington Beach dock.

Then she told him they'd almost killed her.

TWELVE

Lucía was wrapped in the fluffiest, softest, most pure-white bathrobe she'd ever seen.

Ollie sat in the pocket, six of his eight stuffed legs hanging out.

Her hair was still wet from the shower, not even combed, flopping down on her shoulders like Ollie's profusion of legs. Her pair of sweats and t-shirt were borrowed from Maria's closet. Lucía had left the Island with nothing. Wicket said they had everything she needed, not to worry. When Joe met her at the harbor and whisked her back to the cottage, she believed it.

She had the camera. That's what counted.

Now, sitting in the living room in Joe's chair, everyone bustling around her, she just felt... *numb.*

The slight buzz in her limbs was either after-effects from nearly suffocating to death or simply emotional exhaustion.

Joe was next to her, watching her with that attentive gaze of his, but not saying anything. Letting her stay quiet. She was once again interrupting cozy time, but she didn't have the energy to worry about that. She wasn't even sure she should stay. That thought had been nagging at her since halfway across the water. Miller had the coordinates of the cottage. He had to know where she would go first. If he—or Astra or whoever else was involved—was bent on killing her, wouldn't they come here? Why didn't Astra simply let her drown on the ramp?

It all seemed so crazy. What secret could possibly be worth killing over?

She was putting everyone else in danger. There was no way she could stay now. No way Jex or Wicket would want her to, and even if they did, she just *couldn't* do that. Not to them. She couldn't let her bad luck ruin their fairy tale. But that would be it. She wouldn't have to imagine the heartbreak because it would have arrived. The final hit. The one that would crumble everything into the sea.

That thought fuzzed out her brain, making it buzz just like her body. Her eyes closed of their own volition. She couldn't think about that right now. She needed time to recover. Maybe stay the night. Tomorrow, she'd figure out where to go next. What to do.

She was pretty sure she was in shock.

Her eyes opened in time to see Jex arriving with a plate of some incredible pastry and a cup of tea, and that was the thing that did her in. The tears just leaked out. She couldn't even hold the cup, her hands shook too much. Joe took it and balanced it on the arm of the overstuffed chair, holding it near for when she was ready.

She wiped the tears away and tried to pull herself together. *Tea.* The damn tea always got her.

"Maybe you should go rest," Joe said softly. He'd been freaked-out when he met her at the dock. She'd been a shivering wreck in her wetsuit. He'd wrapped his jacket around her and hailed a ride to bring them home, peppering her with questions until he understood what had happened. Then he went quiet, just holding her until she was home and could clean up.

Jex towered over her, concern on his face, not retreating to the kitchen like he normally would. "I have some good drugs."

A laugh erupted from her, short and a little manic. "I'm good. I mean... I'm not okay, but I will be." She pulled in a breath. Somehow saying the words made it more concrete. She'd survived. She wasn't anywhere near okay, but she was alive.

Jex snagged a hard-backed chair and sat facing her. "So, you think this is all connected to our battery backups?"

She lifted her eyebrows and dashed a look to Joe.

"You don't have to talk about this now." He scowled at Jex, who gave him a look like *What?* Joe leaned closer. "I told you, you're the most interesting thing around here."

"You've been telling them?"

"It's what I do." His smile was gentle. To Jex, he said, "She needs some rest. And we should be talking about how to keep her safe."

Jex scowled right back. "That's what I'm trying to figure out." He peered at her, checking her out. She honestly had no idea how bad she looked. "But you can go upstairs and rest."

"It's all right." She didn't want to be alone right now, which was strange—*alone* was just her normal state. "And we need to figure this out." She couldn't do that on her own, not in her current state. "I know it's only been a week, but if you've had more outages, that would be important to know."

"No, they've stopped," Joe said, but his tone said

he was still doubtful about her condition. "Nothing since you told Miller about them."

"So, he's definitely involved." Jex's eyes narrowed like he was thinking about roasting Miller on a spit for his channel.

"It has to go higher than him." Lucía took the cup of tea from the plate Joe was balancing and held it in both her hands. The shaking had settled. The warmth of the cup infused her palms. Just holding it was good enough for now.

"Why do you think that?" Joe asked.

"The power cables." She blew on the tea, sending the steam of it evaporating away, then took a sip. Black and strong, just how she liked it.

"What about the power cables?" Wicket asked, cruising into the room. He'd just padded down the stairs. "There are fresh sheets and towels in your room," he continued without missing a beat. "And Maria is picking out a few more outfits for you, plus pajamas. She'll lay them out on the bed. You just pick which ones you like or keep them all. That girl would rent out part of your closet if she could—she's a fashion *hound.* And do you like that lavender shampoo in the shower because that hair of yours is too beautiful. You must have something special you use for it.

Especially with all that swimming you do! There has to be some kind of product or treatment for that. We'll get you whatever you need, sweetie. You just tell Wicket what it is, and I'll get you taken care of."

"I'm okay, Wicket. I'm good." She smiled, and the tears were threatening again.

"Well, sure, of course, you are." The strain at the corners of his eyes tugged at her. She didn't want to cause them to worry, but that he *was* worried threatened to break her in the best way. "Okay, forget about shampoo." He waved that off and eased up behind Jex, gripping the back of his chair. "Tell me about the cables. There's the extra one, right?" He dashed a look to Jex, who nodded. It was like they'd been following her drama all along. "That's how they're stealing our power, the bastards," Wicket said. "I'm sure someone's making money off that. They should be in jail."

She nodded her agreement, but no way it could be that simple. "Laying down undersea cable is a huge operation. It didn't really sink in until I was down there." Joe, Jex, and Wicket were rapt. "A museum keeper couldn't swing that. I doubt even Miller could, not in secret anyway. Not to mention that it's got to be highly illegal."

"How long has the cable been down there?" Joe asked.

She frowned because that hadn't occurred to her either. "It's not new. Long enough that it's covered with the usual sea life."

Jex leaned forward, lacing his fingers. "How long does that take?"

"Months? Maybe a year? Once it reaches a level of coating, I'm not sure you could tell just by visual inspection. Or in the pictures. It could have been there longer." She glanced at Joe. "I got pictures of the replacement VIV parts, too. Those were brand new."

He'd taken custody of the camera at the boat and still had it tucked under his chair. He dug it out and handed it over to Wicket. "It's an old kind of storage media. We should make copies. Not online, though."

"I'm on it." He took the camera and hustled out of the room, taking a path through the kitchen to his tech-filled office in the back. He was probably happier doing something, anyway.

Maria came down the stairs so quietly, Lucía was surprised to find her in the room with them. "Baby's asleep! Okay, chica, all your clothes are set. But if you look better in them than me, we're going to have some words."

Lucía managed a smile. "Thank you."

Maria went to get a chair and bring it for the little circle forming at Lucía's end of the room.

"I really appreciate the clothes," Lucía added, then to Jex and Joe, "and everything else, I just... I don't know how long I should be staying."

"You're staying as long as you want to stay." Jex's determination made it hard to object.

But they should know the risk. "Miller has the coordinates to the cottage. He knows where I must be. This thing is... big. And they're tampering with the mainland grid AI? I suppose someone could sneak that in, but the cable, the fire, all of it together? I don't feel right dragging all of you into this."

"Last I checked, I live here, too." Jex's anger was still simmering.

She couldn't parse what he meant. "Sure, but—"

Joe's hand touched her arm, just a short squeeze. "I know that tone of voice. That's Jex getting ready to murder someone. Don't give him more reason to."

She was still confused.

Maria waved at Joe. "Jex wouldn't hurt a fly. Unless that fly landed on one of his pastries, then *Adios, Fly!*" She straightened her scrubs—she was still in her hospital gear with *Maria Gonzalez, RN* embroidered on it—and settled in her chair in a way that spoke of long-time fatigue. "What he's saying, chica, is that nobody messes with the cottage. These assholes are stealing power. Do you know what that would do if it hit the hospital? It hasn't, but who's to say that's not next? And I've been out in this neighborhood..." She wagged a finger at the closed blinds behind Lucía. "Mrs. Williams is on an oxygen concentrator at home. Do you know how stressed that poor woman gets when the power goes out? She's got three reserve tanks now, just because. And poor Mr. Nowak? He uses a power lift to get in and out of bed. You going to shut that off for an hour? Two? What if he has to pee? His neighbors take care of the backup battery, but still. What if they're not home? So, no—you're not dragging us into this. We are *in it* already."

Which wasn't at all what she meant, but Maria had a point—whatever this was, they were all impacted.

Wicket trooped in from the kitchen with her camera. "All backed up, and duplicate copies made. Who are we sending this whistleblower information to? Because I have a few things on my mind I'd like to tell them." He handed the camera back to Joe, who tucked it under the seat again.

Before Lucía could even think how to answer

that, the front door swung open, and Amaal and Yorum hurried in. Amaal led the way with her statuesque presence, dressed in a striking red suit that was both professional and creased like she'd been wearing it all day. Her headwrap was as creative as ever, like a tiny red-and-gold hurricane on her head.

"Would have been here sooner," she said, striding over to stand between Jex's chair and Maria's, "but I decided to collect Yoram along the way."

"I asked you to pick me up!" He was dropping his backpack in the hallway.

"It is the same difference." Amaal clasped her hands together as if she were suddenly calling the meeting to order. "Have we begun?"

"Begun what?" Joe asked, but he looked like he knew the answer already.

"To solve Lucía's problem, of course." Amaal dipped her head to Lucía. "If you want our help, that is. I shouldn't presume." But then she kept going, not waiting for an answer. "But it is obvious what we need to do."

"What's that?" She truly had no idea what Amaal was thinking.

"Clearly, this attack is unacceptable." Amaal's bearing took on a hardness, determination sharp in her dark eyes. "They are trying to scare you, and because you are not the kind to be scared, they are trying to eliminate you. I understand people such as these. They are not to be underestimated. But you are talented. You must keep working as a power engineer because we all need smart people like yourself doing that work—the world needs it—and so we must find someone who can protect you and solve this mystery, all this business of stolen energy and fires and illicit power cables. This is obviously not okay, as well."

Joe leaned forward in his chair. "What did you have in mind?"

Lucía was too stunned to even ask that question, but all eyes were on Amaal like they fully expected she had an answer to back that up.

"Yoram," she said definitively.

"Yes?"

"You are the answer."

"I... am?" He looked to Joe, who just shrugged. Yoram turned to face Amaal, who towered a good five inches taller than him. "Do I want to know how?"

"You have that internship, do you not?" Amaal asked, but again didn't wait for an answer. "And your mentor is the Regional Director of USEC for Los Angeles."

Yoram's eyes went wide. "I've met with her precisely one time for five minutes during the interview. I don't think I'm even supposed to bother her again... like, she's handing me off to someone else."

"But you know her," Amaal insisted. "You can contact her."

"I suppose." Yoram frowned as the idea seemed to settle in.

Lucía wasn't sure either. She'd gone to the regional director in Oregon, but this was different.

"How do we know she's not involved?" Yoram asked, voicing Lucía's immediate concern. "Wouldn't it make sense, if something was happening, if this really is some kind of corruption in the power grid management, that she would be involved?"

"We will have to take that risk." Amaal turned to Lucía. "Unless you have a better idea."

She didn't, actually. And she was too tired to come up with one, at least at the moment. "I don't want Yoram to lose his internship over this."

Amaal surprised her by kneeling down in front of her chair and taking her hand. "Lucía," she said softly, "I know this is hard to see, but this isn't just about you, although you are certainly on the front lines at the moment. This is something terrible that's being done to everyone. It affects all of us. And it will take all of us, doing what we can, where we can, to stop it. There is risk. You know this, of course. You have seen it first-hand. But the risk is not only to you. Let Yoram do his part." She half looked over her shoulder. "Am I right, Yoram?"

"I can always get another internship." He actually seemed proud of that.

Lucía's mind was fuzzed out, scrambling to keep up. This was a problem. She should be able to fix it. But she couldn't, not by herself, and here they all were saying—no, *insisting*—they would help. She should say no. She was putting everyone at risk.

Only... she wasn't. She wasn't the one stealing power. She didn't lay down illegal cable or burn down secret labs. Whoever was doing this, *they* were the ones putting everyone at risk.

And that had to be stopped.

Amaal was right. They had to do this together.

It made her terribly nervous—but then this whole thing did. "Okay." It sounded weak, so she added, "Thank you." This was the right choice. It still made a shiver run up her back.

"All right. Good." Amaal climbed back to

standing and straightened her skirt. "Now," she said to Jex, "I think it is time."

He nodded, but again, Lucía had no idea what it was time for.

Amaal tilted her head to Jex and Wicket. "You should do the honors, naturally. But we should adopt Lucía, obviously, and right now. Bring her under our protection."

Adopt... "Wait, what?" Lucía nearly spilled her tea straightening up in the seat where she'd slumped.

"You are one of us, no?" Amaal asked.

"I... would like to be..." She was literally on the edge of her seat now.

Jex was gesturing something on his display. A message popped up on hers. She swiped it open, along with everyone else in the room.

A formal adoption agreement. It was just a script. The real agreement was verbal after voice print. She'd only done it once. She tapped to join the proceedings. Her heart was behaving erratically.

"Wicket, you should start," Jex said.

"I, Wicket Strong, being of sound mind," he recited for the online attorney AI, "do legally agree to the adoption of Lucía Ramirez into the Family Strong. In family, we pledge to care for one another, for better or worse, in sickness and in health, until that bond is legally dissolved by a court of the state of Southern California."

Amaal went next, repeating the vow, and Lucía just sat there, holding her tea, staring as Amaal made the formal pledge online... They were adopting her in without even a discussion. Each member of the family had to agree—it had to be unanimous. Did they talk about this before? Had they already decided?

Her hands shook so much the tea slopped over the side.

Joe gently lifted the cup out of her grasp. "It's okay."

"Did you tell them to..." How could he have talked them into this so quickly?

He smiled. "You honestly think I'm in charge here?"

"Maria?" Jex asked.

"Well, of course, I do!" Maria tapped her display and intoned, "I, Maria Gonzalez, being of sound mind..." She went on, and Lucía's heart was a small bird, fluttering confused in her cage, excited, exuberant... and afraid. Did they really mean it? Were they just bringing her in because they felt they had to? Was there a difference between those that mattered?

Yoram went next.

Jex lifted his chin to Joe. "How about you?"

"Oh, hell yes!" he shouted.

Lucía burst out with a laugh, then it froze in her chest as Joe turned to her, his eyes intense the way they'd been that first time. "I, Joe Paxton, being of sound mind and a great deal of enthusiasm do legally agree to the adoption of Lucía Ramirez into the Family Strong. In family, we pledge to care for one another, for better or worse, in sickness and in health, until that bond is legally dissolved by a court of the state of Southern California." He held her gaze through the whole thing.

"All right," Wicket said. "We're clearly going to have to have a discussion about dating within the family."

"Oh, *come on,*" Joe complained. "I know family comes first."

Wicket jabbed a finger at him but left the rest of the threat unspoken.

Jex rose from his chair and extended his hand to Lucía. He didn't want to shake, he wanted her to get up, so she took his hand, and he helped her rise.

Then he held both of her hands in his two. "I, Jex Strong, being of sound mind..." He repeated the entire pledge then tipped his head. "It's only valid if you accept. And if you're not ready, we'll understand. But if you're part of this family, Lucía, we're not just talking about sharing Basic. It's not just chores or even cozy time. We will do everything in our power to protect you in this. Your fight is our fight. Our home is your home." He slid a sideways look to Joe. "That one knows the rules." Then he faced her again. "Do you accept?"

She was a mess. The tears were just running down her face. "Yes," she managed to get out.

He squeezed her hands. "Then make it legal, dear." And he released her.

She sniffed and wiped at her face. She should *say* something—something nice about how it was an honor and she loved them all already and she couldn't believe they would do this for her, especially given they barely knew her. But all those words didn't mean as much as the ones she actually read off the script. "I, Lucía Ramirez, being of sound mind, do formally accept this adoption into the Family Strong. In family, I pledge to care for all of you, for better or worse, in sickness and in health, until that bond is legally dissolved by a court of the state of Southern California." And then she reached up to hug Jex, and that started a cascade of everyone smushing in. Wicket and Jex squished her between them, then Joe and Maria to the sides.

Amaal's long arms reached halfway around the group, and Yoram stood on tiptoe and patted her on the head. It dissolved into laughter and silliness, and Lucía wasn't sure if she'd ever had a moment so filled with pure happiness. She was floating on it, and it pulled her up out of the shock that had buzzed her body and fuzzed-out her mind. Belonging wasn't a *where,* it was a *who*—and she belonged here, with these people. Even though it was messy and under the strangest of circumstances, it felt right in a way she couldn't put into words, so she didn't try.

But then all of it swam up to her head and made it float. She nearly teetered over, but in the midst of the hugs, it was impossible to fall. Still, Wicket fussed over her and broke up the party, officially calling off cozy time and sending her upstairs to rest, making sure Joe walked her up to her room. Her body felt heavy, but her heart was soaring, and her head was floating. It was the strangest of feelings, and Joe was obviously worried, holding her arm, steadying her in an almost ridiculously protective way, like he seriously thought she was on the verge of collapse.

But she wasn't. Even though her body had absolutely no idea what to do with the emotions zooming through her, the ground felt steadier than it had in a long, long time.

When they arrived at her door, Joe released her, but he still looked super concerned. "Are you sure you're okay?"

"I'm much better than okay." She hugged him, which she hadn't properly been able to do before, and whispered, "Thank you. For all of this."

"You overestimate my ability to get things done." But he was smiling when she pulled back from the hug. She stopped, close, her fingertips on his cheek. She held his gaze for a moment and decided she had no reason to wait. Her kiss was light, but she stayed long enough for him to react, kissing her back. Sweetly. Tender. Like he wasn't quite sure this was happening. Or that she wasn't still going to fall over.

She understood it completely with no words at all.

When she pulled back, his eyes were lit up. "Was that a *thank-you* kiss?" he asked. She could see how much it affected him.

"That's an *I'm trying to date you* kiss." She smiled then backed into her door, opening it behind her. "I'll be all right, Joe." The truth of that settled deep. "Good night."

"'Night."

She closed the door then listened for his soft footsteps away.

Lucía couldn't begin to stop her smile, so she didn't try. But sleep was an urgent need. Her body was deflating, all of everything catching up to her. Tomorrow, they would figure out the next steps. Take what evidence they had to Yoram's contact, the Regional Director. Either she would help, or they'd keep going until someone did. They'd fight this all the way to the top, whatever that was, if they had to. They'd figure out what was truly happening at Power Island One, what was behind the stolen power, and put a stop to it. *Together.*

She cleared Maria's clothes off the bed, crawled in, then sent a quick message to Tito before fatigue could drag her off to sleep.

I'm going to stay. I'm going to fight this. And I'm not going to do it alone.

That night the dream came true before she'd closed her eyes.

The Nothing is Promised series continues with
You Knew the Price:

Subscribe to Sue's Newsletter
to be the first to know about new releases:
http://smarturl.it/SKQsnewsletter

ABOUT THE AUTHOR

Susan Kaye Quinn is a rocket scientist turned speculative fiction author who now uses her PhD to invent cool stuff in books. Currently writing hopepunk, but her works include SciFi, YA, gritty future-noir, steampunk romance, and that one middle grade fantasy. Her bestselling novels and short stories have been optioned for Virtual Reality, translated into German and French, and featured in several anthologies.

www.susankayequinn.com

Printed in Great Britain
by Amazon

12974474R00123